Lock Down Publications and Ca$h
Presents

Guns Down, Bottoms Up!

Bankroll Mafia

By
LO-LIFE

First Edition 2024

Printed in the United States of America

Lock Down Publications
P.O. Box 944
Stockbridge, GA 30281
www.lockdownpublications.com

Like our page on Facebook: Lock Down Publications
www.facebook.com/lockdownpublications.ldp

Stay Connected with Us!

Text **LOCKDOWN** to 22828 to stay up-to-date with new releases, sneak peaks, contests and more…

Like our page on Facebook:
Lock Down Publications

Join Lock Down Publications/The New Era Reading Group

Visit our website:
www.lockdownpublications.com

Follow us on Instagram:
Lock Down Publications

Email Us: We want to hear from you!

Dedication Page

Okay...Here we go again. My 2nd jump shot. There aren't too many people I haven't shouted out but...

Of course, thanks to the most high. If you didn't place me in the position I'm in, I probably would have never stumbled upon my gift and passion to paint these pages with authentic tales of the street life.

To the twins. Momma and Tita...One of these days I'll put your story on paper. Let the world read about the troubles and the triumph. To my sister Tina..I can't thank you enough, but you'll make sure I try. LOL! None of this would have been possible without you. All those nights sitting in front of the laptop combing through my work...Thank you. To my brother Jr..I know sometimes life is hard, but you're built to last, just like your big bro. Truth be told, you're better than I ever was. To my nieces, nephews and my lil' cousin Niya. Y'all are the next generation. Our only hope is y'all do it better than we did. To my kids. Ja'Koreyon, Honey, DJ and Marcus...I hope one day y'all realize that your dad loves y'all more than anything. If I could give 20 years of my life to go back and do it differently, I would. Big Facts!

To the real woman who inspired this fictional tale. Jasmone. Krystina, Jeanette, Cierra B, Ciera S, Raynisha, Lakiesha, Cherry, Rebecca P, Alexis B, Claudia, Meme, Stephanie, Sinnamen, Shayla, Dominique...It's many more, but these are the ones that stuck around the longest. I'm not mad y'all moved on. At the end of the day, *I* let y'all down...

To Cash and the Lock Down Publications family. Much love and appreciation for giving me this chance to share my passion with the world. It's still a trip to go from reading the content, to contributing. I'm trying to soak up as much game as I can. I'm trying to give the rest of the world a piece of mine. 'til the next episode...

Prologue

She laid in her bunk surrounded by concrete and steel. A place comparable to hell. A place where the nights were filled with screams of fear and rage. The days, bombarded with riot guns and tear gas. She still couldn't believe how she arrived at the California Institution for Women in Chino; San Bernardino County.

How did she go from being one of the baddest bitches in the game and dealing with some of the top bosses in the city to serving a life sentence for something she didn't do? It's crazy how life can be sometimes.

Her thoughts traveled back to her true love. She wished like hell he could be with her right then. No, fuck that! She didn't wish he could be there. She wished they could be anywhere else in the world but that God forsaken place.

A place she was left stranded. No support. All those who claimed that they loved her at one point or another can't even find the time to write. She vowed if she ever got released she would get vengeance on them all. As the noise and chaos seemed to grow around her, she laid back, closed her eyes and reminisced about what led her here.

Chapter 1

4 Years Prior

"Damn, Cuz...Hurry yo ass up. You know we gotta pull up on Danny Boy before I shoot to my T-Lady crib," lil' O told Blue as Blue hopped out the car to go pay for the gas. The two 19-year-olds were from the South Side, 3rd Ward to be exact. Right now, they were on the East, which meant they were *way* out of bounds.

The brighter of the two, Blue, walked into the gas station with one thing on his mind. Snacks and cigars. "Can you give me $20 on pump number 2," he told the white, middle aged male cashier.

Once he paid for his purchase, he headed back to the car. Just then, a red drop top Mustang swung into the parking lot. Inside were two of the baddest females he'd seen in a while. That's why he loved coming to the East. They had some of the baddest bitches in the city... And they were straight up freaks. By the time he made it back to the car, lil' O was already at their necks.

"There goes my bro right there," lil' O says to one of the females as Blue's walking up. "Say, Cuz...This right here is Chassidy," he said pointing to the driver. She was bright skinned, long hair with green contacts. "And this her cousin Tasia."

Tasia was more Blue's speed. Red bone, thick as hell with a face like Lauren London. "What y'all 'bout to get into?" Blue asked while licking his lips seductively at Tasia.

"Shit, it's whatever. We're both grown, so y'all tell us," Chassidy sassed.

Both fellas looked at each other. *Danny Boy gone have to wait!* 30 minutes later, they were at the Scottish Inn getting blunted and drinking. Somehow the girls had convinced them to strip down to their boxers and socks.

"Why y'all still got y'all clothes on?" lil' O slurred as his eyelids began to close.

Blue laid across the bed, struggling to lift his head. His whole body felt like a block of cement. He realized something wasn't right. His heart slowed, but it boomed like a bass drum.

Blue began to panic. His eyes were the only thing he was able to move. It seemed as if the rest of his body just wouldn't work. The girls replaced their smiles and giggles with frowns and menacing scowls. They nonchalantly gathered their belongings, made their way out the door as the two men laid there struggling to make sense of the situation, throwing up the East before they closed the door behind them.

Shortly later, the door to the room opens. In steps the last person they expected to see. They whimpered and tried to scream, but it seemed as if their mouths weren't working. The dark figure approached the bed. "Look what we have here. You boys are all the way out of your jurisdiction... Don't matter. We 'bout to welcome y'all properly."

The two began to shake uncontrollably. Now they regretted ever setting foot on this side of town!

Another mid-summer day in the city of Houston. It's a hundred degrees, but the humidity makes it seem a whole lot hotter. You could feel the irritation...The agitation. Everybody's waiting for something to pop off. Greenwood Park was notorious for 3 things. BBQ's, Block Parties and Bodies.

The way it was looking, today would be no exception. Everybody who was anybody was present. Most of them belonged to one of the many crews that terrorized the East

Side streets. If they happened to be solo, well today they may have to choose a side.

It had to be close to a hundred people in attendance. All dressed in their summer's best. At center court, some of the best ballers in the city were immersed in an intense pick-up game. The intensity was only matched by the amount of money that's being waged. Even so, no one seemed to be paying any attention.

All eyes were locked on the drama that seemed imminent between two of the worst crews in the city. On one side of the court, you had Brandon "Bankroll" Banks and his ruthless crew called the Bankroll Mafia. Even though he was only 23 years old, he was the undisputed boss and everyone knew it. He sold dope, but his crew specialized in everything from murder, extortion, bank robberies and commercial burglaries, AKA "going in".

Even though he's a Blood, his crew consisted of Crips, Folks and even a couple Hispanics that repp'd Tango Blast when they were in prison. Brandon felt what you repp'd didn't determine if you were real or not. He judged each individual according to their actions. His crew, in his eyes, were the best of the best. Certified Gangstas!

On the other side of the court, you had OG Paccy and his crew. The Insane Guerilla Family. Anyone who knew them knew they were just that. Insane! According to the streets, you had to have a body to be able to rep the IGF logo. Supposedly, Paccy had 10 himself. Their gun game definitely was the truth, but they weren't getting any real money.

No connect wanted to do business with them. They had a reputation for robbing and killing their plugs. Most of their money was made by kicking in trap spots and extorting drug dealers.

The beef between the two crews started behind what most do. Women! This particular woman is as bad as they come. Standing at 5'6", caramel skin with wavy black hair. Chrissy had a body that would have been sure to give Fred Sanford a heart attack. Size 26 waists, 40 inch ass, Double D tits and a pair of hazel green eyes that would have your dick hard just gazing into them.

She moved to the East when she was really young. Like most chicks from the suburbs, she was infatuated with the streets and the niggas who ran them. Matter of fact, a hood nigga was her second addiction. Her first... Money! That's exactly why the two men were in the situation they were in.

2 months ago, Chrissy was at the Galleria when she bumped into a hood nigga who got her juices flowing. She didn't know who he was, but unbeknownst to her, he knew exactly who *she* was. That was the reason he felt he had to have her.

Walking out the Gucci store with her hands full, she spotted him and a couple of his homeboys hanging around the food court. She had never cheated on Banks. Well...Not for free. A while back, this dude offered her 2 grand to suck on her pussy. Of course she couldn't pass that up. After she came twice on his lips, she figured fuck it and let him pipe her down. She didn't count that as cheating though.

She had to admit. That tall, dark chocolate nigga was sexy as fuck. Him and Banks were around the same height. At 6'2", where Banks would be considered a red nigga, he was midnight black. Chrissy did a quick appraisal of his assets. He sported a Cuban Link chain and what appeared to be a custom King Johnny watch, fresh white tee, Gucci cargo shorts and a pair of $350 customized Jordan sneakers. Those were the same ones Chrissy had planned on getting Banks before she left the mall. He noticed her sizing him up and took that as an invitation.

"What's up, lil' momma? I noticed you eyeing a boss, so I figured I'd introduce myself."

Cocky, Chrissy thought. Just how she likes them. Too bad she had a man already. "Naw. I can't lie, you're sexy as fuck, but I already got a man. I guess you can say I was... Window shopping."

"Why window shop? What, your man can't afford to give you enough for what you need," Paccy capped. He pulled out a thick knot that appeared to be nothing but hundreds, fifties and twenties.

Chrissy looked at the stack and her pussy instantly began to pucker up. First thing she thought about was those gold and black Louboutin's and that new alligator Fendi bag she had been eyeing. Even though Banks would have gotten it for her eventually, he was too reserved with his cash. She wanted it now and not when her birthday came around. She bit her bottom lip, gazed into his eyes and said, "So what you got a lil' knot? If you ain't trynna spend to win, then you're in the wrong game."

Paccy was no stranger to tricking. He considered it paying for convenience. He wanted to fuck who he wanted to fuck, how he wanted to fuck and when he wanted to fuck them, without the added stress of them blowing up his phone in the middle of the night. Especially while he was laid up with his wifey Tasha. "Girl, you ain't saying nothing. What's it gonna cost me? A band?"

Chrissy looked at him like he had lost his mind. "A band? The only thing a band will get you is a whiff of this pussy once I make myself cum. You'll need 3 bands to ride this ride. If you ain't got it, it's cool... I understand. Y'all niggas be having to use your whole roll on y'all reup or whatever, but if that's the case, you should have left it at the house. Real ballers only floss their spending money."

He loved a sassy chick and Chrissy was making his dick jump, but he wouldn't back down. "First of all, baby girl, 3 bands ain't shit to a boss. I pissed that out after a long night at the club. But check it, though. If I spend 3 bands, then I want it all. Pussy, head and ass. Oh, and for the record... I sell dope in my free time. I'm what dope dealers call the boogeyman, but you can call me Paccy."

Once Chrissy heard his name, she finally understood the situation and the danger it entailed, but it was already too late to back out. Hell... She didn't want to. After their little exchange, she figured he might have some good dick to go with them 3 bands she was about to get out of him.

One thing for sure, she had to make sure Banks never found out about it. He would kill them both. Under no circumstances could she allow Paccy to figure out who her man was. Hopefully, he never asks.

After a little more conversation, they decided to dip off. Paccy had her follow him to one of his spots so he could get lit first. His drug of choice was wet. Especially when he was about to fuck a bitch down.

15 minutes later, they pulled up to the Choice Inn on Maxey Road. Paccy went in and paid for the room. The Arab behind the counter smiled and gave him the key to room 137.

While he was paying for the room, Chrissy's phone rang to the tune of Rick Ross. *I'm the biggest boss you done seen so far.* Of course, she knew who it was before she answered. "Hey, boo," Chrissy sang. For some reason, Banks always had the worst timing.

In that deep drawl of his Chrissy loved so much, he asked, "Where you at?"

"Oh, boo...I'm at the mall still. I'll be home in a couple hours. Why? Is something wrong?"

"Naw. Everything good, baby. I just called to let you know I'ma be late coming home. I got some bidness I got to take care of on the southwest, and it may take a few hours," he explained.

"Aight, baby...I'll hit you when I step foot in the house so you'll know I made it home safe," Chrissy chimed.

"I love you, boo."

"Love you, too!" Chrissy hung the phone up, placed it on vibrate and dropped it in her purse. She loved Banks with all her heart, but she really didn't look at what she was doing as cheating. To her, she was hustling just like he was. Only difference was, her pussy was the drug and she had an endless supply. No droughts.

Soon as the door closed, Paccy was all over her. With handfuls of her soft plump ass, he sucked and nibbled on her earlobe. That was her spot. She could feel her juices begin to dampen the crotch of her True Religion jeans. She pushed him onto the bed and began a slow, sensual strip tease for him.

First, her top. Then, her bra, revealing a pair of perfect melon size breasts. Next, she undid her Gucci belt and sashayed out of her jeans. Behold...The prettiest, fattest, pinkest pussy Paccy had ever seen. He couldn't help but to lick his lips as he stared at heaven on earth. The wet he smoked earlier had his dick hard as a steel bar. What he craved right then and there, though, was a taste of her essence on his tongue.

"Come ride my face."

She hopped onto the bed and slid her pussy across his mouth. He noticed a faint trace of peach body spray. Her juices dripped down his chin as he tried feverishly to suck and swallow up every sacred drop. As he nibbled, sucked and assaulted her clit with his tongue, he pushed his right thumb into her booty hole to loosen her up.

"Ooohh, ssshhiit! Fuck! Suck that pussy, nigga," Chrissy moaned with pleasure.

Paccy knew exactly what needed to be done. He slowly began to fuck her asshole with his thumb until he felt her body begin to tremble.

"Ohh my… Gawd... I'm 'bout to cum… Fuucckk! Don't stop!" Chrissy began to tear up at the sheer pleasure Paccy was delivering. He picked up his pace. Stabbing at her backdoor with his large digit. She began to grind her mound against his face. Her asshole clenched around his finger. He knew she was cumming. "Oh shit..! Here it cums. Eat that nut, babbbyyy!"

Chrissy came so hard Paccy had cum all in his nose. Not to be outdone, she slid off his face and worked her way down his body until she was face to face with his 8-inch, heavy duty dick. With the tip of his cock touching her nose, she looked him dead in the eye. With one swift motion, she had most of his tool stuffed inside her mouth. Paccy moaned and grunted. Chrissy knew she had him.

With no hands, she worked her neck and tongue, leaving his dick fully saturated. She worked him with both hands. Massaging his shaft as she sucked on the head like a King Size Blow Pop. Just when he thought it couldn't get any better, she dove headfirst under his nut sack, sucking each testicle as if it were a ripe mango.

"Fuck...! Damn, girl. You a straight up freak!" Paccy announced. He didn't want to cum so soon, so he had her get on all fours. Grabbing the Magnum out of his pants pocket, he rolled it on and slid deep into her wet coochie. Even though Banks was packing a healthy 9 inches of dick, Paccy punched into her with so much force, she had no choice but to try and get somewhere. "Uh Uh...Where you think you going? Bitch, you gon' sit here and take all this dick," Paccy taunted.

Chrissy looked back at him with a sneer. "Oh, that lil' thing? Nigga, my tampon bigger than that!"

Even though both of them knew Chrissy was just talking shit, it didn't stop Paccy from putting a serious beat down on her coochie. He was amped up off the juice. Going long and strong. Sweat dripping, muscles bulging. His dick breaking down her walls. After she came for the third time, he pulled out and slid up in her ass. He *loved* pussy, but it was something about fucking a bitch's asshole that did something to him.

Sure enough, after about 20 strokes into her backdoor, he felt his balls churning and burning. "Oh, shit. I'm 'bout to cum... Catch this shit!" Paccy growled.

Chrissy pulled off the dick and turned around, just as Paccy was snatching the wet condom off. Without warning, warm dick milk shot everywhere. Her face, her hair and even her eyelids. Whatever was left, she licked it up, making sure the dick looked polished. After all, if a man spends 3 grand, he deserves to be cleaned up after the mess.

Paccy collapsed onto the bed. After a blunt of Exotic Loud, he fell fast asleep. As soon as she heard him snoring, she crept out of bed, headed to the shower to clean up.

Once she was done, she dressed, collected her money then was headed out the door when something caught her eye. Paccy had his pants draped over the chair by the window. Her mind flashed back to the knot he had shown her earlier. She tiptoed, then searched through his pockets. *Bingo!* She quickly stuck the knot in her purse, ran out the room, then jumped in her car.

As soon as she got home, she counted the money. *15 grand!* Who would walk around with that much money on him? "Oh, well. He shouldn't have gotten caught slipping," she whispers to herself as she prepares for bed.

When Paccy did finally wake up, it didn't take him long to figure out what happened. He was irate! He knew he couldn't tell anyone what happened. One, he'd be the laughing stock of the East and, two, his wifey Tasha would be sure to find out, and he wasn't trying to deal with those type of problems.

Ever since then, he had been searching for a legitimate reason to have beef with Banks. He even had a few of his homies go around calling Banks a snitch, hoping he would retaliate. So far, nothing!

As he stood there watching Chrissy hanging all over Banks, he wanted to go over there and tell him how good her head and pussy was, but that would lead to everyone finding out he had gotten burnt for his bread. *Damn!* He was pissed but had to be patient. Something will happen. It always does!

Chapter 2

Banks stood and watched Paccy mean mug him from across the court. He didn't know what made the nigga drop salt on his name, but then again, a nigga didn't need a reason. They hate just because. He also noticed his girl Chrissy was acting kind of strange. Ever since they arrived at the park, she'd been acting nervous as hell about something. Maybe it was due to the tension, he reasoned. As many situations as they had been in, she should have already known he wouldn't let anything happen to her. He made a mental note to ask her about it later.

As he studied her features, he had to admit Chrissy was shutting the park down. He had the baddest bitch on the East. Hands down! Draped in an all-white Fendi dress that was hugging her curves like it was hanging on for dear life, red and white Fendi heels, white Fendi tote bag, and of course, a pair of Fendi shades. Forget the East. She might be the baddest bitch in the city. Big Facts!

"Boo, I wanna suck that big ole dick of yours. How 'bout we burn off and go get a room real quick," she whispered into his ear, licking around his lobe.

Immediately, his dick began to swell at the thought, but he couldn't leave just yet. Not in the middle of a stare down. It would make him seem as if he bitched out...And *that* was out of the question. "Baby...A nigga can't leave right now. Especially while my niggas are still here and these bitch niggas plex'd up like this."

Of course Chrissy knew that was going to be the answer. She had to try anyway.

Ever since she saw Paccy at the park, her stomach had been turning flips. This was the first time she'd seen him since she burnt him for his paper. Now that he and Banks were in the same place, she was scared to death. She needed to get her nigga as far away from the park as possible. She was pleasantly surprised that Paccy was keeping it playa. Even still, she felt the daggers he shot at her with his eyes. She just prayed Banks hadn't noticed them also.

As she tried desperately to figure out a way to lure Banks away from the park, his right-hand man Killa walked up and whispered something in his ear. Banks listened attentively, looked at her and then frowned his face up. *Oh my God...Killa just told him*, Chrissy thought.

A few agonizing seconds ticked by, Banks did a double whistle, signaling his crew to mount up. She breathed a sigh of relief. She knew if he had found out, he would have given his crew the signal to "hammer" everything in sight. Closed fist to his palm. At least they were leaving. Whatever the reason, she was grateful.

Banks owned a couple whips, but he had pulled out his 2023 candy red Escalade on 28" Forgi's. The inside was alligator with suede trimming. Out of all his cars, this was his baby. Mainly because this was *Chrissy's* favorite truck. Every time she got in it, she couldn't help herself. She had to give him some sloppy top, or some of that wet, tight pussy. That's what she had planned on doing soon as they hopped in the truck.

"Boo, I'ma drop you off. I need to go handle something."

She knew whatever Killa had told him must have been serious. She usually would have pressed him to go on, but decided not to this time. She had an eerie feeling deep in her gut. She grabbed his hand and demanded his attention. "Look at me, Brandon. Baby, I love you so-so much. Please... Make it back home to me." They had been together for 6 years. Ever since he was 17 and she was 16. They knew each other, inside and out. And she knew he was on the way to go put in some work.

"Don't I always make it back home?" he said. "Plus...We need to have a talk when I get back." Little did she know, Banks had planned on proposing at the park in front of the whole hood. Whatever had come up forced him to postpone it until later. He wanted to set it up so it would be memorable and special.

If he would have known about Chrissy's dirty little secret, there would have been no way he would have embarrassed himself like that. He loved Chrissy, but if he ever found out, he'd have had no understanding, and she'd have been dead as a doorknob.

Last year, he had hooked up with a real estate agent by the name of Cierra. After 4 hours of mind-blowing sex, she was ready to do *whatever*. She helped him get the 4 bedrooms, 3 bath, brick home he and Chrissy shared. She also helped his right-hand man Killa get a home out in the Woodlands. Just on the strength, Banks let Killa fuck her while she sucked on his dick.

Banks always had "the gift". He could get a person to do anything at any time with anyone. He and Killa were the closest of friends. They shared everything. Well...Except Chrissy. She was the only one off limits.

After Chrissy slid out the truck, Banks hopped in his low-key whip. A black 2018 Chevy Impala. Everything factory. Tinted windows. He pulled his phone out and dialed Killa's number.

"What it is, Blood?" Killa answered.

"I'm on the way...Get everybody ready," Banks responded.

"Ovastood!" With that, Killa hung the phone up. The conversation lasted no more than 20 seconds. That's how it's always been between them. Straight to the point. Never would they incriminate themselves.

Banks scrolled through his playlist. He searched for his favorite mixtape. "Blow". *I Can't Feel My Face* by Juelz Santana and Lil' Wayne. As the four 12" Folsgates thumped, he reminisced on the day he and Killa became friends, and eventually like brothers.

He was 12 years old, and his family had just moved to Houston to avoid the gang-infested streets of Baytown. Due to his stepdad being a drug addict and a con man, their apartment was shot up in broad daylight. Luckily, no one but his stepfather was injured. Shot in the head. Died on the scene with half his brains on the welcome mat.

Unfortunately, his mom had a nervous breakdown because of it. To help her out, his aunt brought him to live with her and her husband on the East Side of Houston.

The neighborhood he was from in Baytown was named Northwood, AKA "The Beehive." Before he left, OG Butch told him when he turned 13, he could come back to the hood and they would "Bleed" him in. Until then, he could only rep Blood Gang since he wasn't on an official set yet.

His second day in his new neighborhood, he threw on his tan Dickie shorts, his red and white All-Star Chuck Taylor's, a red shirt and his red and white snapback with the Boston Red Sox "B" on the front. He picked up his basketball and took off down the street, eager to find out what his new neighborhood and city was all about.

So far, everything seemed quiet. That is until he came upon a group of kids playing basketball in the middle of the street. Once one of them spotted him, they gave the head nod and everyone else turned their attention to the new guy. A dark-skinned kid who seemed to be the oldest pointed in Brandon's direction.

"Where you from, my nigga...Cali?"

Brandon paused and thought about the comment, trying to decide if it was intended to be an insult or what.

"Why you dressed like that?" another kid asked.

Brandon looked at himself. *Dressed like what*, he thought. "Naw. I'm not from Cali. I'm from Northwood. The Beehive," he repp'd.

They all looked at each other, assessing the situation. They all had heard stories of the infamous Beehive, but none of them were old enough to venture into the neighborhood themselves. For all of them, Brandon was the first person they'd met that claimed to be from there.

The self-elected spokesman for the click was named Freddy. He was named after his big cousin Freddy C from McNair. McNair is a notorious Crip hood that laid on the other side of I-10. They were the ops and even though he had family there, Freddy's mom would never allow him to go visit. Because of that, he could never be in the hood to be able to get officially "put down".

Since Brandon was claiming to be from the ops, Freddy looked at it as a chance for him to put in some work for the set. Being the so-called leader of the band of misfits, he came up with the idea for them to jump Brandon. Everyone in the click was down with the idea. Except for one.

His name was Joshua King. He would later be given the name Killa King and he had very well deserved that title. Even though he was short in stature, he made up for it with strength and determination. With skin the color of Onyx stone and eyes that already precluded the madness that would soon follow, Killa was already an intimidating figure in the neighborhood.

At 12 years old he was already playing with various handguns. On this particular day, his weapon of choice happened to be a .38 he " borrowed" from his older brother Melvin.

Without warning, 3 out of the group converged on young Brandon. Now, one thing about Northwood...The older homies always made the younger ones fight each other. Regardless if y'all were cool or not, they still made y'all fight. So, to Brandon...A fight was as normal as breathing. He hated getting jumped, but he was no stranger to it. He was ready!

The first one made a move and swung a wild punch. Brandon ducked up under and hit him hard in the nose. He felt the bone crunch and knew it was broken. The kid hit the pavement screaming, blood pouring through his fingers as he covered his nose. Now it was down to 2 against 1.

This time, both kids rushed in. Brandon tried to fight them off best he could, but they were bigger and stronger. After a few seconds, he was being pummeled. He kept repeating to himself, *Don't hit the ground...Don't hit the ground.* He knew once he hit the ground, it was all over for him. They would be sure to stomp him out.

He wasn't sure how long he would be able to stay standing. Just when he thought he was about to pass out, he was only getting hit by one pair of hands. Then, all of a sudden, the hitting stopped. He picked his head up. The other 2 kids were both laid out cold.

Banks wasn't sure if Killa was a friend or foe. He squared up and got into his fighting stance.

Killa smiled and stuck his hand out as a sign of friendship. "They call me Lil' King," he said.

Banks looked at his outstretched hand and shook it. "My name's Brandon. Everyone calls me Lil' B," Brandon replied.

Killa looked at the front of the snap back laying on the ground. "Is that why you wear the hat with the B on it," he inquired.

"Well...My hood's all Bloods and we wear stuff that represents that."

Killa looked at him with a new sense of respect and admiration. "So...You're a Blood?"

"Not yet, but I will be next year when I turn 13," Brandon answered.

Killa had always been fascinated with gang life he saw on TV, but this was the first one he came across in real life that was down or at least affiliated. He made up his mind right then. If they allowed him, he would become one, too.

They shook hands and since that day, they have become inseparable. A year and a half later, they both returned to Northwood, and with OG Butch's blessing, they both got down with the set. Everything was shared. They even lost their virginity at the same time with the same girl Crystal, who happened to be Brandon's girlfriend at the time. When he was 14, he convinced Crystal, who was 18 at the time, to have a threesome with him and Killa. When he turned 16 and had gotten kicked out of school, his uncle kicked him out of the house, and he started sleeping on the floor in Killa's room. He would leave right before his mom got up for work, and as soon as she left, he would come back.

When they needed money, they would go out and rob just to have enough to last a week or two. Then Brandon met a Mexican chick named Mona. She would change their lives forever.

Mona was very pretty. Brown eyes, long hair and a nice set of titties. Her ass wasn't all that fat, but she had enough to hold her own. She had always seen Brandon around and knew from the first time she laid eyes on him she had to have him. When she found out how old he was, that didn't deter her at all. She saw it as a chance to groom him into the boss nigga she needed him to be.

Even though Brandon had a few experiences with girls at that time, nothing compared to Mona. She was the first to swallow his seeds and his young mind was blown away. By her being 24 years old, she knew things he couldn't fathom. She taught him how to please a woman. How to eat pussy until she screamed and creamed on herself. She taught him how to fuck a bitch into submission. Most importantly, she taught him about the dope game.

Her whole family was into selling dope. They had family members that were deep off into the Cartel. Kilos were purchased for a little bit of nothing. She taught Brandon how to cook dope, repress bricks and how to stay low key while doing it. After a night of passionate sex, she gave him the nickname he would forever go by.

"As long as you're with me, you'll always have a bankroll," she told him as she massaged his limp and exhausted dick. Her older brother Raul had G'd for the young hustler, and even though he was low key racist, he had to admit it. Brandon was growing into one solid motherfucka!

As the head of the family, Raul was in charge of the shipments. He made sure everyone was paid and they received what they were supposed to. When he started to get fond of Brandon, Mona felt like it was finally time for Brandon to step his game up.

Until then, he was flipping 4 and a halfs, and 9 packs. He wasn't tripping, because he was only 16 and pushing a late model Cadillac ATS on 84's with candy paint and suede seats. He rocked a $20,000 watch and his chain cost the same. Add to all that, he stayed putting that shit on!

Before he dropped out of school, he was "that nigga" on campus. Even still, Mona wanted more for him. She knew he could be legendary in the game. She approached Raul with a proposition.

"Raul, I think he's ready," Mona said while standing by the door of the money room.

Raul had given some thought to bringing Brandon up a few levels, but he still wasn't sold on the idea. He knew that his baby sister's emotions might just well be clouding her judgment. "Why do you feel I should just invest our family into him? He's not La Rasa. Plus, he doesn't seem like he wants to handle the heavy weight," Raul explained.

"I know he's ready and willing. Plus, I'll be right there. It's not like we won't have eyes on him," she countered. "Look at it this way...If he fucks up, I'll take care of him."

Raul stared at her a moment before replying, "Do you really believe you could do what needs to be done? We both know that you're in love with him." She looked down at her feet.

After a few heartbeats, she found her voice to respond. "Yes, I do love him...With all my heart, but if he betrays our family...I won't hesitate to kill him!"

Raul saw the sincerity in his baby sister's eyes. He nodded his head. With that, Raul agreed to start fronting Brandon bricks of coke. Everything was flowing smoothly. 2 months later, Mona had been gunned down. Retaliation for one of the hits her brothers carried out on their rivals.

Brandon was crushed. Mona was the first woman he truly loved besides his mother. A few weeks after the funeral, he sat in his Lac at 2 in the morning reminiscing. As he fought back tears, drinking on a bottle of Hen, his phone began to ring.

"Hello," he answered with a heavy slur, 2 shots away from blacking out.

A familiar voice came through the headset. "I need you to meet me at my Tio's."

"Okay," Brandon answered and the line went dead.

Raul wanted Banks to go to the same spot he made his pickups. He wondered why. He had just picked up 5 birds a couple days ago. At the current rate, he was taking about 3 weeks to get rid of that much work. Mainly because he was cooking a lot of it. Whatever Raul wants, he'll make sure that he's there to find out.

When he arrived, he noticed 2 black Suburbans parked in the driveway. He realized that he recognized them. They were only used to put in work. Brandon had an eerie feeling when he hopped out the car, but Raul was practically family, so he assumed he was safe.

As he entered, he saw 2 older Hispanic males sitting on the opposite side of the living room. Raul stood in the center with a black beater, some tan dickies and a pair of Cortez Nikes on. His cell phone pressed to his ear. When he saw

Banks, he told the caller he would call them back. "Que Paso, B? How you been?" Raul asked.

"Trynna hold it together, big bro," Brandon answered.

Raul stared at him for a while before he spoke. "I have great news... We found my sister's killers."

Brandon's ears perked up at the mention of Mona's killers. He immediately became sober. "Who was it?" he asked anxiously.

"These motherfuckas from the Southwest. The Cholos. We know where they're at right now, but I need *you* to handle this. Can you do that for me? For this family? For Mona?"

Without hesitation, Brandon said, "Hell Yeah! Just tell me where they're at, and I'ma twist their shit back!"

Raul smiled. "Si. My sister loved you, and I see now that you love her."

That night, Banks caught his first 2 bodies. Up until then, he had shot at plenty of dudes, not really trying to hit any of them. This was the first time he stood over someone and watched as he extinguished the life force from their eyes.

Right afterward, he went to the tattoo shop and got Mona's name inked across the top of his back from shoulder to shoulder. He looked to the sky with tears in his eyes. "I will always take you with me wherever I go."

Chapter 3

A while later, and a month before his 18th birthday, he met Chrissy. He was just leaving the courthouse, fresh from beating a fluke ass pistol case. She had been at court to support her brother Charles. He had gone on trial for a manslaughter charge and had been found guilty and sentenced to 20 years. Chrissy was in tears. She and her older brother had been very close.

Banks saw her distraught and approached cautiously. "Hey...Excuse me. Are you alright?"

Chrissy looked up through red, puffy eyes and said, "Please leave me alone. I'm not in the mood right now."

Banks felt that if she wasn't so upset at that moment, she would have been more receptive to his charms. He took a few seconds to choose his words wisely. "Look, momma, I don't know what's gotten you so upset, but you're just too damn gorgeous to be out here crying your eyes out like that. If you give me a chance, I want to make this the last time you cry in pain... If you change your mind... Here goes my card. Hit me up."

Chrissy took the card and stuck it in her pocket. More so to get rid of him, than of interest. He was excited to beat his case and wanted to celebrate. He couldn't keep his mind off the chick he'd just met. Well, technically, he couldn't say he met her, because she never gave him her name. He knew exactly what he needed. He called up Daneesha.

Deenesha was a certified nympho. She loved to fuck until she couldn't walk straight and suck dick until she couldn't talk right. "Hello," she answered breathlessly.

"Wassup? What you 'bout to get into," Banks asked curiously as to whether or not she already had someone else's dick to play with.

"Well, hopefully it's not me that's about to get into something, but you."

"Fa sho," he agreed. "Well, check it. I'm on the way right now, so get ready."

"Bring me something to drink. You know I'ma need an extra boost to handle that big ole dick of yours."

"Don't I always?" With that, he hung up and headed to the liquor store. He snatched a bottle of Hennessey off the shelf for him and a bottle of Alize for her. He copped a quarter ounce of Sour from the lil' homie Fitz, and a box of condoms.

When he pulled up to the apartment complex, he spotted a group of niggas shooting dice in the breezeway. He had an urge to get out, get down and try his luck, but decided not to. He had his mind on some good ass pussy and right now he wasn't about to let nothing deter him.

He honked the horn. A few moments later she emerged. He couldn't help but to admire how bad she was. If she wasn't a downright nasty ass freak, he might have wife'd her. He loved freaks, but he needed one that could be loyal to *him*. He didn't feel as though Deenesha fit the description.

She was a high-yellow chick with a nice fat ass, slanted eyes, some juicy titties and a pair of luscious full lips. She wore her hair in a ponytail, but it still came down to her lower back. She had a yellow sundress that came mid-thigh and was damn near see through. You could tell by the way her ass cheeks jiggled with each step she either had on a thong or no panties at all.

His dick already stood at attention, anticipating what was to come. Even though she was a freak, she always kept her

27

pussy tight and her hygiene in tip top shape. As she opened the car door and hopped into the passenger seat, Banks got a whiff of her perfume— "Nude" by Rihanna.

"Damn, girl. Your ass smells good enough to eat," Banks stated with a smile.

"Boy, don't start with me," she shot back. They had been messing around for 3 months and Banks had yet to nibble on her cookie, due to the fact she felt his remark was done sarcastically. Little did she know today would be the day.

He was on cloud 9 and was down for the whole 9. "I got you today, girl...That's on the set. A nigga trynna turn all the way up today."

"Yeah...Whatever... We gon' see. A bitch can suck your toes, lick your balls, but you don't ever want to sip on this hundred percent fruit juice I got for you," she states as she flips the visor down to check her makeup.

When they got to the room, they poured up a few shots and blew 2 blunts. As Banks finished off the last blunt, Daneesha began to crawl towards him. She reached into his Polo boxers and fished out his rod.

"Damn," she whispered to herself. She could never get over how big his dick was. It had to be 9 or 10 inches long. The head was the size of a peach, with a big, pulsing vein running down the middle of it. Every time he put that dick on her, she could feel him all in her throat.

"Ssshit!" Banks hissed as she devoured everything in front of her.

She massaged his balls as she sucked on his plum-sized dick head like he had the fountain of youth buried deep in his nut sack. She felt his cock harden, jerk and knew he was moments away from cumming. She picked up the pace, jacking his dick rapidly.

"Agh...Agh...Ohhh, sshit...I'm 'bout to cummm!" Banks howled.

"Shoot it down my throat, daddy," was her reply.

Backs grabbed the side of her head, tilted back and roared as he unloaded so much cum into her mouth she couldn't swallow it all. Excess nut dripped from the corners of her mouth. After she scooped and swallowed it, Banks informed her that it was now *her* turn.

She couldn't believe what she was hearing. She was finally about to feel those sexy ass lips on her pussy. He laid her down, pushed her legs back. Her pussy laid bare, opening like a flower in bloom. He leaned in and began to suck gently on her clit. Her juices ran profusely down his chin. He took his middle finger, stuck it in her cunt and scooped up enough lube to puncture her asshole.

"Oh shit! Oh shit! That's it...Give it to me, baby. Treat me like the slut that I am," she begged. Banks inserted his index finger and used that to massage her g-spot. That drove her over the edge. In less than 5 minutes, he had her cumming all over herself. "Ooohh shit...Ooohh ssshhiitt! I'm cumming...I'm cumming. What the fuuuccckkk!" she screamed. Her body convulsed, then collapsed. After her orgasm subsided, she hit him on the shoulder.

"Ouch! What the hell was that for?"

"Nigga! You mean to tell me, you can eat pussy like that and you had a bitch waiting months to get her shit done right?"

Banks just laughed at her comment. "So what? Are you ready for another round?"

"What? Hell yeah! What type of question is that? A bitch trynna leave outta here in a wheelchair!"

They went at it all night. By the time they were done, Deenesha had made up her mind. As long as Banks kept giving her this type of dick, then he could get whatever, however, and whenever he wanted. She knew he had money, but she would give him her life savings to have him for life. Banks, on the other hand, drove home thinking about the girl at the courthouse.

***

Banks pulled up to the spot and noticed Killa's all black Charger on 22" Lexani's parked behind Bizzy's candy red Buick Park Avenue on 84's. They were his second and third in command. Rarely were they ever seen together. That would defeat the purpose after all. Tonight? Well, tonight is different.

Less than a month ago, some unknown assailants tried to run down on Banks and rob him. What they weren't expecting was for him to be strapped and willing to dump on them in the middle of traffic. Even though no one was hurt, Banks said he wouldn't stop until he found out who tried to play him for prey. Finally, he had names to go with the faces. Soon as he walked in, Killa wasted no time.

"Say, Blood, the homies on the South Side say them niggas were from the Tre. They was just some young niggas who bit off more than they could chew. Basically, they thought they saw something weak. They didn't know who they were fucking with," Killa added.

Banks grimaced. Then a slow smirk developed on his face. "So, let's show them, then."

With that, Killa made the call. Banks walked to the door and he could almost smell the fear permeating from the room. Strapped to two metal folding chairs were 2 frightened 19-year-olds. Their hands, mouth and feet were duct taped. You could tell that neither of them knew why they were there. The last thing they remembered was lying up with a couple of freaks they met at the gas station earlier that day. Now, they were down to their boxers and socks, strapped to chairs in a pitch-black room. They heard the doorknob twist and turn open. A glimmer of hope pulsated through their bodies. Maybe someone had come to set them free. All that changed when they saw the face of the last person they expected to see.

"So…You two lil' niggas are the ones that had the bright idea to try and rob the next king of the city," Banks spat.

Both youngsters pleaded with their eyes for mercy. It was futile. After their botched robbery attempt, they had told their big homie Stank about it. Based on the description they gave him, Stank knew exactly who it was they tried to rob. He told them they needed to finish the job. If not, it would be only a matter of time before Banks would come calling. Even though he was considered young, he was already being hailed as a legend in the hood. He also started to gain respect and notoriety from his peers across the city as a ruthless G! Even though the pair didn't know who Banks was at the time, they were about to find out.

Banks looked at the two with disgust. "I know you two lil' niggas might not know who I am, but y'all 'bout to go to hell screaming my name forever."

With that, Killa and Bizzy came into the room with canisters of gasoline. Upon seeing this, both teens started shaking violently in their seats. One even urinated himself as he begged for mercy, screaming out his lungs through the duct tape. Now, they wish Banks would get it over with and just shoot them in the head. To Banks, that would have been too easy. He wanted to make a statement that would reverberate throughout the city.

As he watched the gasoline being doused over the two, his phone vibrated. He glanced at the screen and saw it was Chrissy calling. He turned his back to the gruesome scene and answered the call. "Hello?"

"Heyy, babe…Are you aight?"

"Yeah, baby, I'm good, but I have to call you back. I'm kind of busy right now." Banks tried to rush her off the phone.

"Umm…Before you hang up, how long before you get home," she asked suspiciously.

"Why? You plan on going somewhere," he replied with a slight attitude. He didn't know if he was tripping, but it seemed Chrissy was acting real suspicious lately. He would hate to have to kill her behind some grimy shit.

"Well...Dorian had called. She wants me to go to the club with her. Sooo, I told her to come scoop me up, unless you're tripping. Then, I'll just stay home."

Brandon thought about it, then replied, "Naw...You good. Do you. I'll catch up with you later." Then, as an afterthought, "Do you have some money?"

"Yeah, I got a few bands on me. Plus, you know I ain't 'bout to pay for shit." She wanted to add *I'll get them niggas to pay for everything*, but caught herself and instead said, "Dorian will pay since she's begging for me to come with her."

"Aight... I'll talk to you later," Banks said before he hung up. Something about the whole conversation threw him off, but right now he had more important things to worry about.

He turned back towards the frightened and bewildered teens. He watched as the tears poured from their eyes. Without so much as an ounce of empathy, he reached into the pocket of his Robin Jeans and pulled out the same piece and chain he had on the day they tried to rob him. The ironic thing was that the chain was the least expensive piece of jewelry he owned. Since they traded their lives for it, he felt it was only right they took it with them to the afterlife. He draped it over one of their necks and whispered into his ear, "When y'all get to hell, let them bitch niggas know that when I get there, it's still *up* with us." He gave Killa a subtle head nod, turned around and walked out of the house.

Within seconds, he hears the agonizing sounds of flesh burning to a crisp. He didn't need to wait to see the results. He never did. Killa was proficient at what he did. After all, he was dubbed Killa K... The Executioner!

Chapter 4

"Biitttccchhh! I'ma kill them hating ass hoes tonight," Dorian screamed through the phone as she eyed the outfit she planned on wearing to the club.

"What you pulling out," Chrissy asked with interest. She wasn't about to let Dorian outdo her.

"Naw. Naw, bitch. Not this time. You gon' have to sit your high-yellow ass over there and try to guess what I'ma come with," Dorian chided. Last time she made the mistake of letting Chrissy know what she had planned on wearing earlier that day. Chrissy hightailed her size 40 ass to the mall and came with a Versace dress that shut the party down. *No bitch! Not this time,* Dorian thought.

"Girl, stop tripping," Chrissy shot back. "We're both going to be killing it tonight. I just want to see if maybe you wanted to coordinate on something." Chrissy was hoping that she would at least tell her what colors she planned on rocking. Almost every time they go shopping, they go together. Chrissy knew just about every piece of article Dorian had in her closet.

"You're not slick, C," Dorian mused. "I'll say this. My shoes will look like I walked through a puddle of blood."

Oh. This bitch gon' pull out the Lubies, Chrissy mused to herself. Lubies was the nickname they gave the famous Christian Louboutin heels. Chrissy thought for a few seconds and instantly knew what Dorian had planned on wearing. *I got something for her ass... Checkmate!*

33

"Well...Let me go get dressed. I don't know 'bout you, but I'm trynna have something loooonnnggg and hard to ride at the end of the night," Dorian sang as she did a lil' shimmy in her seat.

"Bitch, you know Banks would kill me if he even *thought* I was stepping out," Chrissy admitted.

"Chrissy, you know Banks gon' fuck him something before he comes home. Shit, he's just like his no-good ass patna Killa!"

About a year ago, Chrissy and Banks attempted to play matchmaker by hooking Dorian and Killa together. After about 3 months, the situation turned into a disaster. Killa felt that Dorian wasn't nothing but a sack-chaser. He never had any intention of trying to wife her. Unbeknownst to everyone, Dorian only agreed to fuck with Killa in hopes that he would run back and tell Banks how good her pussy and head was, prompting Banks to want to try it for himself.

Banks always knew in the back of his mind that he could have Dorian anytime, anyway he wanted. He respected Chrissy too much, plus he would never shit where he slept. Dorian wasn't bad looking at all. In fact, she was one of the baddest females on the East. Standing at 5'4", cocoa brown skin, fat ass and perfect C cup titties, she had a set of lips like Yandy from Love and Hip Hop. When she wore those skintight boy shorts, you can tell her other pair of lips were just as juicy; maybe even juicier.

She and Chrissy had been friends ever since first grade. Even though Dorian loved Chrissy, she secretly envied her. That's why she made it her goal to always fuck on Chrissy's boyfriends at least once. So far, Dorian has had a perfect record. Well, until she started messing with Banks. She knew Banks was attracted to her. She caught him staring at her ass a couple times when Chrissy wasn't looking. She couldn't figure out why he hadn't slid up on her and tried to slide up in her. Until he did, she would never stop trying. Fucking Banks was becoming an obsession of hers.

"Girl, you're too much. I'ma holla at you when I'm ready, so you can come scoop a bitch up. I'm glad you're driving though, because I plan on getting lit as fuck tonight. And you know this...Mannnnn!" She imitated the character Smokey off *Friday*. She hung the phone up, then hopped in the shower, intent on showing Dorian how to leave them haters dead.

By midnight, they were headed to Club Heat downtown. Dorian was killing the scene in her all-white Valentino body dress, gold Louboutin pumps with the white crystals on them, gold hoop earrings, and a white and gold Louis Vuitton clutch. Not to be outdone, Chrissy stepped out in an all-black Michael Kors skirt with the inverted white blouse. She was sporting so much cleavage she could have taken an eye out. Black Balenciaga thigh high boots with a white and black zebra print Gucci clutch. Of course, neither one had on any panties.

As they pulled up to the club in Dorian's cherry red 745LI, all eyes were on them. They loved going to Club Heat because they never had to wait in line. All they had to do was get the club owner Big Tuck on the phone, and not only were they escorted in, but they would be able to reserve a VIP table of their choice.

Tuck had been sniffing at Chrissy's goodies for years. She never allowed him to get even so much as a whiff. She pulled out her phone, scrolling through the contacts. When she got to his number, she pressed call.

"Ayyeee." A deep, grizzly bear growl came through the receiver.

"Heyyy, Tuck. We're outside, baby." She could hear music playing in the background. He had to be in the office because the music wasn't as loud.

"Go ahead and come in. Tell Uno to give y'all a couple bottles and head over to VIP booth number three." Before he hung up, he added, "Say, Chrissy?"

"Yesss?"

35

"Do you got any panties on?"

"Come on, Tuck. You know they just get in the way." With that, she hung the phone up. She knew Tuck wanted her worst than he wanted air to breathe. She never gave it to him because he wasn't her type, and most importantly, he was cool with Banks. Or so Brandon thought. It always amused Chrissy to see Bank's so called patnas get at her the minute his back was turned. The crazy thing is, they know Banks is retarded, but they still try him.

As soon as they stepped into the club, they felt it was going to be a hell of a night. The place was jammed packed. Bodies were everywhere. The club was definitely jumping. The bouncer and manager Uno approached them and asked where they would like to be seated. "Booth number three," Chrissy replied. Then she remembered the bottles. "Oh...And send two bottles of Ciroc...On Tuck!"

Uno disappeared, and the girls made their way to the VIP booth. Before they made it to their seats, Chrissy noticed something bling in the corner of her eye. Sitting in the booth right next to theirs was the sexiest nigga she had ever seen, next to Banks.

He had to be 6 foot something, chiseled frame, peanut butter complexion with light brown eyes. What stood out the most though was his hardware. The man was definitely on disco ball status. With a quick appraisal, Chrissy estimated his neck, wrist and fingers to be anywhere between 80 to100K...Easy!

Her pussy instantly began to leak. He must have sensed her squirt. At that very moment, he looked up and caught her gazing at him. He smiled and she damn near came on herself. *Damn! This nigga's definitely my speed. Too bad I'm already taken!*

The sexy stranger wasted no time. He sent a bottle of Rosé to their table, requesting that *"the two lovely ladies accompany him in his booth."* Even though Chrissy wanted to, Dorian declined and he respected and accepted it. Yet and still, every now and then, they would search for each other's eyes.

"Damn...Banks gon' have to beat this pussy up tonight. This nigga got a bitch running hot," Chrissy mumbles to herself as she fantasizes about the stranger. She never even noticed when Dorian got up and headed to the dance floor.

25 minutes later, Dorian was popping and twerking her ass all over some dark chocolate brother with real good, curly hair. His hands were on her hips while her ass cheeks gripped the sizable print in the front of his slacks. Chrissy smirked to herself. She knew for sure by the end of the night Dorian would be stuffed full of chocolate cock.

Chrissy sipped her drink idly. Suddenly she felt a huge presence towering over her. Staring down from his 6'6" frame, Big Tuck smiled. His gold and invisible set diamond teeth sparking in the club's lights. With a smile so seductive he spat, "Damn, Chrissy...You looking good enough to eat... And I'm a man with enormous appetites."

Normally, Chrissy wouldn't have entertained him, but the stranger had her simply ready to explode. She couldn't wait to meet up with Banks later on. She had an idea. "Well, Tuck...You know in order to eat well, you have to pay well. How much are you willing to pay so you could eat at the buffet?"

Tuck looked at her in disbelief. Was he finally about to get a chance to suck on Chrissy's perfect peach? "Chrissy, I ain't gon' lie. My tongue is long. My dick is longer, but my money's the longest of them all. So, *you* tell me what you gon' hit my pockets for?"

She thought about it for a few moments. She knew she couldn't let him gut her out. She had a man to go home to. She was almost certain Banks would want some pussy when he came home. "Two stacks for a snack," she challenged.

"Bet!" Tuck quickly agreed, hoping she wouldn't change her mind. "Meet me in my office." Then, Tuck walked off.

Chrissy thought about letting Dorian know what was going on, but then again, why bother? It shouldn't take long for Tuck to have her flooding everywhere.

As she walked out the booth, she took one more glance at Mr. Sexy. He motioned for her to come to him. She walked over to his section. As he stood up to greet her, she got a whiff of his Armani Code Cologne. Her knees started to become weak. He handed her a business card and proceeded to walk off without a word. *Damn...Ain't that a bitch!*

She glanced at the card. It read *Saint Lucian* in gold writing. Plus, a phone number was printed right below the name. She dropped the card into her purse on the way to Tuck's office. Pussy juices running down the inside of her thighs.

Soon as she walked in, she noticed that the lights were dimmed and the sound system in the office was apparently different from the clubs. She and Tuck were jamming R. Kelly while the club was screaming, "Turn down for what!"

Tuck sat behind his giant mahogany desk. It appeared that he must have swiped everything off it because the contents were all littered on the floor. The only thing on the desk was a neat stack of bills.

Chrissy smiled and seductively sashayed over to him. She picked up a stack and discreetly did a flip count before dropping it in her purse. She laid her purse on the couch, walked around the desk and stood directly in front of Tuck.

Tucks breathing became labored as she undid his belt and fished out his elephant trunk of a dick. His cock felt warm in her tiny hands. His heartbeat could be felt through his giant vein. As his member began to grow in her grasp, she had to admit to herself Big Tuck wasn't lying when he said he was BIG. His shit had to be 11 inches and growing. There was no way she was about to let that monster of a cock run up in her. Banks would surely know the minute he slid in. Tuck would remodel her insides. The freak in her wanted to try, though. *Fuck it!*

Before she could say anything, Tuck pushed her back against the desk. She looked at him and bit her bottom lip. Little did he know, she liked it rough. Getting manhandled got her going. Chrissy felt daring.

"Tuck, if you can make this pussy skeet in less than three minutes, I'll let you stick that big ole dick anywhere you want... Free of charge."

That's all he needed to hear. Tuck snatched her forward until her ass was hanging off the edge of the desk.

She looked at her diamond studded Rolex, waiting on the second hand to finish the revolution and end up back at 12. "Go!" She urged.

Tuck dove in headfirst. She honestly didn't think he could accomplish such a feat, but the minute his tongue touched her clit, she realized she might be in trouble.

Tuck sucked, nibbled and licked on her nub. With 2 fingers, he massaged and plucked at her G-spot. Her juices began to pour out the seams of her fat ass cat, dripping heavily onto the wooden desk. She began to sweat. Her temperature elevated. It couldn't have been more than 2 minutes and she was on the verge of exploding. She fought it off, but he was relentless. The tip of his tongue assaulted her clit with back-and-forth swipes and figure 8's while her fingers vandalized her sweet spot. Her orgasm built to dangerous levels. She didn't know how much longer she could withstand it, but still she fought. Sweat cascaded from her brow as she squirmed under the pressure of pleasure.

Just when she thought she had it tamed, he stuck his left thumb in her booty hole and Chrissy lost it. She came so hard she had tears in her eyes. "Ooohhh! Fuuuccckkk, Tuuccckkkk!" She squirted streams of her essence all over the man's face. Every time she thought the tremors subsided, she would get hit with another and small squirts of cum would spurt out. "Fuck! Shit! Man, I just came hard as hell," she confessed breathlessly. She looked at her watch. Lucky for her, Tuck had taken 3:12 to get her there. She didn't think she could handle another one like that, but damn, she wanted to try. She looked down at Tuck. He was gently nibbling on her outer lips. *Damn...This nigga's head game is off the chain. I wonder what his dick is like.* "How 'bout one more for the house," she whispers.

Without a second thought, Tuck began his assault again. She came so hard the second time her body locked up and she was temporarily paralyzed. He looked up at her with a greasy chin. All he could do was smile. "Damn, Chrissy. You got the best tasting pussy a nigga's ever had!"

"For two grand, it better be," she replied as she fixed herself. She grabbed her purse and took one more look at the tree trunk hanging between his legs. *I probably would have came just by sucking that big motherfucka!*

"If you ever need it again, don't hesitate to ask," Tuck told her while tucking his dick back into his slacks.

"Would that be the nut or the cash?"

"Both," he said with a chuckle as she walked out the door and back into the club.

As soon as she returned to VIP, Dorian rushed up to her. "Damn, bitch! Where you been? I'm ready to bounce. I met this sexy ass nigga named Rico. We 'bout to hit the room. He got a homeboy. Wassup," Dorian utter excitedly.

"Naw, I'm good, but you know how we do. I'll ride with you so I can hold you down."

"Okay. That's a bet. Let me know."

Dorian and Chrissy were like 2 dudes when I came to sex. A lot of times, when one was headed to fuck with a dude for the first time, the other would tag along as a chaperon/bodyguard. Most times, they would be right there in the room watching the other get their freak on. As long as they've been doing it, not one of the dudes ever complained about having a 3rd wheel in the room. Why would they? You're fucking a bad bitch while another bad bitch watches.

Pulling up to the hotel, Chrissy catches a glimmer in her peripheral. *Damn, it's Mr. Sexy...What did the card say? Oh yeah. Saint Lucian!* She noticed he wasn't alone.

Walking in tow there were 3 exotic looking women. She sat and watched them strut out of the hotel lobby and pile into a candy red Bentley truck. She had to ask herself, *What the hell he got going on?* Chrissy felt enchanted. She made a mental note to definitely contact him soon. She needed to figure out what type of timing he was on. She had been faithful to Banks so to speak, but this man is dangerous with a capital D. He looked like he could have a bitch strung out on the dick and thirsty for his drip.

"Bitch...Did you hear me?" Dorian said irritably. She assumed Chrissy had been listening, but quickly found out that was not the case.

"Huh? My bad, girl. What'd you say?" Chrissy asked sheepishly.

Dorian smacked her lips and shook her head. "See, you don't be listening. I asked what time you tryna take it in tonight?"

"It can't be too late, D. You know Brandon would have my head if I pull up later than him. He usually pulls up around 4:30," she admitted.

"Okay...Well it's 1:30 right now, so we can bounce around 4 o'clock, then. That will give me two hours to get my cookie eaten and beaten," Dorian jokes.

They both erupt in laughter, giving each other high fives. They parked and entered the lobby. Rico was at the bar waiting for them. Once he bought rounds for everybody, they made their way to the elevators.

As soon as they entered the room, Chrissy excused herself and went into the bathroom so she could call her man. He didn't answer. She texted, waited for a response, then called again. When it never came, she used the restroom, washed her hands and returned to the bedroom.

As she stepped back in, she immediately heard the unmistakable slurping sounds of some top-grade head being administered. Sure enough, Rico sat with his back against the headboard. Dorian was on her hands and knees, positioned between his legs, eating him alive!

It seemed like every time one of the girls was watching the other, the one in the act always turned it up a notch. Since elementary school they've been competitive. Chrissy knew she was in for a hell of a show. She pulled up a chair, sat down and prepared herself to enjoy the performance.

Every now and then while Dorian was polishing his knob, Rico would glance at Chrissy. He could tell the scene was making her wet. Knowing that had his shit on extra brick.

Dorian continued to devour his cock while she massaged his balls. Spit flew from the corners of her mouth as she bobbed, shoving his dick as deep as she could muster. She wouldn't dare gag. Not while Chrissy watched. Chrissy was a deep throat diva who rarely ever gagged on the dick, so neither would Dorian. She felt his balls tighten and knew he was soon to explode. She sped up her pace, in love with the taste of cum. She needed him to beat the pussy up long and strong. Getting that first nut out the way was a good way to ensure that.

As if on cue, Rico announced with a growl, "Damn, D! You 'bout to make a nigga cum down your throat!"

That seemed to turn Dorian up. She picked up her pace to a fevered pitch. Opened up her neck to full capacity and allowed his shaft to fit snugly as she worked her neck muscles. Hot nut splashed against the back of her throat, but she didn't miss a beat. With 3 nice size gulps, she made all traces of his cum vanish. His dick head became sensitive. He attempted to pull out, but Dorian locked on like a mad pit bull refusing to let him go. After begging for release, she finally did.

With a soft pop, his dick fell out her mouth. She wrapped a condom around it and climbed on top of him. "Ooh, shit!

Boy, you got a big dick," she moaned as she began to bounce on it, coating his cock with honey glaze. "Fuck this pussy, baby...Dig it out," she urged him on.

Rico flipped her on all fours, pushing her head into the mattress. He took his dick head and rubbed it from the crack of her ass down to her sopping wet slit. With one forceful push, he buried his cock deep into the root of her pussy. Dorian let out a shriek but bit her lip to suppress her screams.

He slowly stroked her. Making sure to keep eye contact with Chrissy who was rubbing her clit vigorously. Rico picked up the pace. With a thumb nestled in her backdoor, he pounded her guts out. *Squish! Squish! Squish!* Her twat was so wet it felt like Rico had his dick inside a water balloon.

"Fuck! I'm 'bout to cummmm! Damn, Chrissy, this niggas got some good diccckkkk," Dorian howled, and before she knew it, she had her first earth-shattering orgasm of the night.

Rico looked down and saw Dorian's honey slashed against his abs as he continued to stir up her honey pot. He laid her flat on her stomach as he deep-stroked her into a coma. The whole time, Chrissy kept her legs wide and her hands on her pussy. By the end of the session, Rico came twice. Dorian came four times and even Chrissy came once.

Chrissy checked her watch. It was going on 4 o'clock which meant it was time to go. They each said their goodbyes, then Chrissy had Dorian drop her off at the house.

She noticed Banks still wasn't back yet. She went inside, took a shower then called him again. This time he answered. "Hello?"

"Hey, baby...Are you on your way home yet?"

"Yeah... I'm 'bout to pull up right now."

"Good, 'cause momma needs some of daddy's big ole dick," she seductively purred.

"Oh yeah...? Well, I'ma definitely beat your back in tonight!"

"Oooh shit. Hurry up, baby...And I love you."

"I love you too, boo!" Banks said before hanging the phone up.

She was glad she didn't let Tuck run up in her because Banks would have definitely noticed.

As soon as he entered the crib, they went at it. Even though she came a total of 3 times that night, that didn't stop her from cumming another 3 more times. When the sun came out, they were all sexed out. Falling asleep in each other's arms.

Chapter 5

Boom! "U.S. Marshals! Everybody on the ground!"

At first Banks thought it was a dream until he noticed there were real AR-15's pointed at his head. *What the fuck?* His initial reaction was to grab his pistol and go out with a bang. His better, more rational mind told him to wait. Feel the situation out.

This had to be a mistake. 5 burly white dudes were up in his crib with guns as long as his arms, looking to make him another statistic.

One of them approached with the air of triumph. "Brandon Banks. You're under arrest for the murder of Ronald George. You have the right to remain silent. Anything you—"

Bank's head started to spin. He hadn't even noticed Chrissy had begun to scream hysterically. Only thing he kept asking himself was *Who the fuck is Ronald George?*

As soon as he felt the steel cuffs snap around his wrist, he snapped out of his trance. He called Chrissy's name. She was so intent on screaming her lungs out she couldn't hear him. "Chrissy! Chrissy," he barked.

Finally, she looked in his direction, eyes filled with tears. Nose dripping snot.

"Call my lawyer and call King, ASAP!"

She nodded her head as the U.S. Marshals forcefully pushed him out of his home and into the Gulf Coast Task Force Suburban.

"Fuck," he screamed as they slammed the backdoor.

"Yeah. You're definitely fucked," the redneck in the front seat chided.

"Naw, motherfucka...Fuck your momma!" Banks shot back.

The Marshal laughed. "Where you're going, they don't fuck mommas, they fuck daddies. Good luck, cocksucker!"

Banks realized it was no use going back and forth with the fool. He just sat back and tried to collect his thoughts.

A few minutes after they escorted Banks out the house, Chrissy finally got a hold of herself and remembered her man's instructions. Her first call was to his lawyer, Joe Bayter. Joe was one of the sharpest, slickest, criminal defense attorneys in the state of Texas. He was young. At the age of 32 he had gone against some of the State's best and had yet to lose a case. He was great at what he did which meant he was also expensive as hell.

Chrissy knew Banks was banked up, but she didn't know exactly how much he had. Hell, she didn't need to know. He always took care of her and now it was her turn to take care of him. Her next call was to his right-hand man.

The phone rang three times then, "Hello?"

"Killa...? They came and got Banks," she frantically said.

"Huh? Say what? Who got Banks?"

"The fucking cops got him. They talking 'bout he committed some murder. Killa...Man, what the fuck y'all done did?" Chrissy needed someone to blame and Killa was bound to be her scapegoat.

"First of all, *we* ain't do shit! Secondly, don't be on the phone talking reckless. I know my nigga taught you better than that. Now, I know you should have already called Joe, so sit tight. Wait until he gets a bond and we'll go from there," Killa spat through clenched teeth. He never really liked Chrissy. He felt she wasn't right for his nigga, plus he knew how her best friend got down. *Birds of a feather flock together.* Due to his relationship with Banks, he respected her and never spoke on how he felt.

Chrissy couldn't do anything else but calm down and wait it out. "He should be getting processed tomorrow. I'll go see him and let you know what he's talking bout," she told him.

"Aight...I'll catch up with you later." With that, Killa hung the phone up.

Chrissy took a deep breath to settle her nerves. *Damn...Just when shit was going good for a bitch, this shit happens.* She waited by the phone all day. She knew Banks would call the minute he made it upstairs.

2 hours later the phone rang. *"You have a collect call from...Pick up the phone."*

Chrissy pressed "0" to accept the call. "Heyy, baby," she sung trying to lighten up the mood.

"Chris...Them hoes got me on a no bond." He got straight to the point.

That little news crushed Chrissy like a ton of bricks. "So. What does that mean?" She was almost too afraid to ask.

"Well...Nothing right now. Joe should be able to get me one. The reason why they got me on no bond, supposedly the witness is claiming that I threatened her life. Since she feels like her life is in danger, the judge signed off on the no bond until a hearing," he said solemnly.

For about a full minute, nothing was said. Then, Chrissy whispered, "I love you."

"I hope so," Banks replied coolly.

"What's that supposed to mean?" she spat heatedly.

"Look, babe, this a different ball game. You ain't never have to do time with a nigga. Before you say anything, your brother doesn't count. Doing time with a brother is not the same as doing time with your man. Out of a hundred chicks who fuck with street niggas, only 2 or 3 actually got what it takes to hold a real nigga down. The way it needs to be done."

"Sooo. What you're saying is I'm not thorough enough?"

"No...What I'm saying is, show me you are." They talked for a few more minutes. He informed her of what needed to be done and reminded her to lace Killa on what steps he needed to take. She wanted to ask him how was she to pay Joe if she didn't know the combination to the safe, but she held her tongue. *When it's time he'll tell me.*

After she hung up, she finished off her glass of Hennessy, then drew herself a hot bath. She really needed to reflect on what Banks said. Could she really hold him down like he needed her to? *How hard is it, really? I mean... I hope he knows a bitch gon' need her cat scratched every now and then, but he'll have plenty pics and letters. Hell, I'll even bring some shit up there, if he figures out a way to get it in... Yeah, I can do that. I'm a Boss Bitch who's wifey to a Boss Nigga. Of course, I can do this.* With that, she relaxed and allowed herself to doze off in the tub.

Joe is one sharp white boy! Banks thought as he watched his attorney swag into the courtroom dressed in a tailor made Michael Kors 3-piece suit, Burberry scarf, ostrich shoes, and a $40,000 presidential Rolex. Joe was by far the flyest lawyer in the city.

"Hey, Banks. What's good," he quipped.

What always stood out about Joe was he never sounded corny when he spoke slang. *He must have been one of those white boys who grew up around blacks.*

"Shit...Nothing right now. I hope you're about to change that," Banks replied.

Joe opened his file, took a deep breath and said, "Look... We've been knowing each other for a while, so I'm not going to bullshit you. This shit looks really bad. Notice I said *looks*. We both know that looks can be deceiving. Right now, they have you on a 1st degree murder. Um...Some dude named Ronald...? Ronald George, AKA Ro Ro. Do you know him?"

Banks trusted Joe with his life, so he knew he could trust him with the truth. "Joe. I swear to you, dawg, I have no idea who that is. I'm anxious to hear you read the report, to see if it jogs my memory, but I doubt it will," Banks told him honestly.

"Well, allegedly he was killed on June 12th, 2022. He was shot in the back of the head with a high-powered caliber round. Most likely it was a .45 bullet. Half his skull was crushed. They supposedly have the murder weapon, which was conveniently buried with him. If that's not strange enough, the murder weapon has a partial fingerprint. But all that, I'm not worried about. They supposedly have an eyewitness to the shooting. A woman named Sharon Sawyer...She said she heard a commotion next door, gunshots, then looked out her kitchen window and saw you leaving the house.

"According to her, you were covered in blood. She called the cops and told them everything she saw, *once* the body was found. Now all that's fine and dandy. What's killing me is *how* they found the body. An anonymous caller told them exactly where to dig."

Banks' head jerked back in confusion. He took a few minutes to let everything soak in. None of it was making sense. The whole play was sloppy, and he knew for a fact he didn't commit the murder. "So... What now? Joe, I need a bond." Banks pleaded.

"Well, I'm working on that," Joe assured him. "That Sawyer woman is claiming she's getting threatening phone calls late at night and that strange cars have been parked on her street. They've just admitted her to the State's version of the Witness Protection Program. They don't change your identity like the Feds, but they keep armed guards around as well as placing the witness in a safe house until the trial is over with."

"Fuck," Banks shouted. He couldn't believe it. *Who the fuck is this nigga?*

Joe gave him a few moments to compose himself. "Look, B, I feel we can beat this. What they have is real shaky and very circumstantial. I need to sink my teeth into it. You know

49

I haven't lost one yet, and I don't intend on starting now," Joe confidently stated. "It's just going to take me a little time to weave through the bullshit."

"How much," Banks asked getting straight to the meat of the matter.

"A 100k before trial and 75 more if we got to go...Which I doubt."

"Almost 200 large for a body I ain't catch?" He had the bread, but he didn't know he could trust Chrissy to grab it. Banks had close to 800K put up. This would take a nice chunk out of his stash, but it was no way around it. He had to pay. Then he had an idea. *Killa should have 100K. Shit, he's been eating just as long as I have.* "Be expecting the bread within the next few days," he assured Joe.

With that, they parted ways. Banks went back to the tank and immediately hopped on the phone. As soon as Chrissy answered, he explained to her about the lawyer visit. She broke down in tears.

"How long will you have to stay in there," she asked between sobs.

"The way it's looking, if they don't give me a bond, probably a year to a year and a half," he replied. He knew a murder case could intake 2 to 3, sometimes 5 to 10 years, sitting in Harris County. He didn't want her stressing, so he gave her the best-case scenario. "Chris...I need you to pull yourself together. You're my other half and I can't have my mind, body and soul crippled. I wouldn't be able to think or get around like I need to."

"You're right, baby... I'm so sorry. I'm supposed to be the one to tell you to get yourself together. To hold your head up and everything will be alright," she cried.

"Baby, I need you to holla at Killa. Tell him I need him to bring Joe a dollar and I'll hit him back later on."

"But...But why don't you just pay him out your stash," she asked.

After a short pause, "Look, just tell him that for me...Aight?"

He doesn't trust me, Chrissy thought. "I'll let you know what he says when I come visit tomorrow," she gritted through clenched teeth. She was truly hurt by the show of mistrust. She held it close to her chest though, and after they expressed their love for each other, they hung up.

She dials Killa's number. *No answer!* She tried it again, but this time she left a message. *"Say Killa...This Chrissy. B said he needs you to let him hold a dollar. He said to bring it to Joe by tomorrow and he'll hit you back as soon as he gets a bond. Call me as soon as you get this, so I can tell him what's up when I go see him. Okay. Bye."* Hopefully he calls back soon. All night she waited on the phone call, but it never came. She finally fell asleep, exhausted from crying all night. That night she had dreams that she was getting married, but in the dream she couldn't see who her husband would be.

Boom! With an explosion, the front door of Banks and Chissy's home caved inwards. Pieces of splintered wood flew everywhere as three masked gunmen rushed in with assault rifles. By the time Chrissy was able to realize what was going on, one of the gunmen walked up to her and backhand slapped her, causing her head to snap back violently as she fell back onto the love seat. Blood stained her white teeth.

"Bitch, if you scream, I'ma leave you right on the floor with a hole in your pretty lil' head!"

Chrissy was so terrified, her whole body shook. She couldn't think straight. "Wh... What do y'all want," she pleaded.

"Where's the motherfucking safe at?"

"It's in the bedroom," she answered, hoping that would suffice.

The gunman snatched her by her hair, dragging her towards the bedroom. Chrissy had only a Scooby Doo Tee shirt and some black silk panties on. Now, the same panties were indecently jammed into the crack of her most private areas, as she struggled with the gunman's grip.

He threw her in front of the safe. "Open it," he commanded.

"I don't have the combination," she cried out.

Smack! Another hard slap to her face. Blood trickled out her nose. "Bitch...Do you think I'm playing with you? I'ma give you one more chance. Open. The. Mother. Fucking. Safe!"

Chrissy began to sob uncontrollably. She *really* didn't know the combination, and now she resented Banks for not trusting her with it. She knew it was a possibility she could lose her life because of that. "Please... I don't know it... I swear. Please, don't kill me!"

The gunman's phone vibrated. He picked it up. "What the fuck is taking so long?" The voice demanded.

"The bitch talking 'bout she don't know the combination to the safe."

"Of course, she doesn't know it, you stupid motherfucker! He wouldn't have trusted her with it," the voice snarled. "Just get the motherfucking safe and leave...That was your orders!"

"Well... I was just trynna save us some trouble. That motherfucka looks heavy as hell," the gunman whined.

"Nigga... That's why I sent 3 of y'all. Say... Stop playing. Get the fucking safe and make sure you leave the bitch alive!" With that said, the line went dead.

The gunman studied Chrissy for a few moments and with a sly smile he said, "Well... Today is your lucky day."

He told gunman number two to hand him some zip ties. With them, they secured Chrissy's hands and feet. She was forced to watch as the three of them grabbed a blow torch and went to work on the safe.

After close to an hour, they were finally able to prop it onto a dolly and wheel it out the front door and into a black Dodge Caravan. Chrissy felt helpless. She just watched as her and her man's savings literally got carted off. *Fuck!*

Right then and there, her immediate problem was trying to figure out how to get out the zip ties. After 3 hours of struggling, she passed out. More from emotional exhaustion than anything.

"Chrissy! Chrissy! Where you at?" Dorian carefully crept through the house looking for her best friend. After a few hours of blowing up Chrissy's phone and getting nothing but voicemail, she decided to just get in her car and pop up. She really thought Chrissy was busy getting her back beat in while Banks was locked up. Dorian was hoping to catch her sideline boo while he was still there. When she drove up and saw the front door caved in, her heart dropped to her stomach. She knew immediately something was wrong. She contemplated calling the police, but it was no telling what Banks might have stashed in the crib. So, against her better judgment, she decided to tip toe through in search of her best friend. "Chrissyyy…? Where you at, girl?" She went into the master bedroom and almost fainted when she saw her girl zip tied, face swollen with caked up dry blood. "Oh my God," she whispered and covered her mouth. Then the realization hit her that they might not be alone. She darted her eyes back and forth. Looking for any signs of unwanted company. Satisfied that they were indeed alone, she ran towards Chrissy, shaking her frantically in hopes that she would wake up. "Chrissy? Chrissy!"

Chrissy slowly tried to open her eyes, but they were practically swollen shut. "Dorian," she croaked.

"Yeah, girl...I'm here," Dorian whispered. "Are we alone? Are they gone?"

Chrissy couldn't do anything but nod her head. Even that caused her to grimace in pain.

"I'm 'bout to call an ambulance."

"No," Chrissy muttered. Her throat sounded parched, but she said it with conviction. "Water," she whispered.

Dorian went into the kitchen, fixed her some water and grabbed a steak knife on the way back. When she returned, she tilted the cup to Chrissy's bruised and battered lips, so she could get a quick sip. Then she cut the zip ties and allowed Chrissy to drink it herself. After getting her bearings back, she told Dorian all about the previous night.

"Damn, D... Banks is going to trip the fuck out when he finds out!" As an afterthought, Chrissy grabbed her phone and attempted to call Killa. *Straight to voicemail.* "What the fuck?"

"Girl, who you trynna call," Dorian asked.

"Killa... I'm trynna see why he ain't answering the fucking phone."

"Girl... You ain't heard?"

"Heard what," Chrissy asked.

"Killa got smoked yesterday. They say he was on the South Side fucking with some bitch and she set him up. They say his car was all shot up. They burned it with his body still inside."

That's why he hasn't been answering, Chrissy thought. Now she definitely didn't know how she was going to break all this bad news to Banks. How the hell were they going to be able to pay Joe? She knew Banks would be calling soon. For the first time, she wasn't looking forward to it!

Chapter 6

Banks laid in his bunk staring at the ceiling. He overhears the news reporting a homicide on the East Side of Houston. Banks' ears perk up. He tries to listen for any clues that could reveal the ones that did the sliding.

Since the news was on, he knew what time it was. He had been waiting on the 2 o'clock count so he could call Chrissy and check on the status. Even though she was scheduled to come see him later that evening, it was no way he could have waited all the way until then.

"Y'all, get ready for chow," a sexy voice alerted over the intercom.

He knew exactly who it was, and he couldn't do anything but smile. Detention officer Tracy Jones was what they called an Amazon. 5'9", 160 lbs. Hershey chocolate skin with bright pink lips. She was built like a young Buffy the Body. She had a habit of wearing her work pants so tight you could see her sex lips poking out like a camel's knuckle. She had a thing for Banks and he knew it. He thought she was cute, but she was only 20, and even though he was only 3 years older, he still felt as though she was still a child. Still, that didn't prevent her from pursuing him.

Banks decided to go ahead, get up and start his day off. He washed his face, brushed his grill and took a piss. He unwrapped his du-rag, hit his waves a few times, then stepped into the day room.

After getting his tray and sitting down, his old school patna taps him, leans in and whispers, "Say, nephew, that hoe sweating you harder than a Sahara sand-dweller. You need to go ahead and get in her chest like Vicks Vapor Rub."

Banks could feel Officer Jones' eyes burning a hole in the side of his head. He played it off. He doesn't look her way, but tells Serve, "I ain't worried 'bout her, Unc...I'm just focused on getting back to the pad. Plus, I got a bad bitch at the house, so I ain't hurting for nothing."

"See... How many times I got to tell you, young playa? Just 'cause you ain't thirsty right now don't mean you can't dig a fresh well. Ain't no telling when the well you're drinking from will run dry," Serve spat.

Banks had to admit it to himself. The old nigga was right once again. He wasn't quite sure how long Chrissy would be able to ride, so he couldn't afford to turn down anything while he was locked up.

Serve was an old school Pimp who caught a murder case in the line of duty. He told Banks it was behind a trick beating and raping one of his girls. "These women are with you for guidance, protection, security, and if someone violates either one of those things, then you must violate them!"

Banks had never thought about pimping, but after being on the tank with Serve for the last few weeks, his interest was piqued. He was definitely thinking about fucking with it.

Serve was a stocky dude. Salt and pepper hair with a small scar above his right eye. He talked smoothly but with authority. It was easy to see how someone could be captivated by his aura and his words. For some reason, he believed Banks possessed "the gift". The crazy thing was, he wasn't the first person to tell him that. Every day, he would drop jewels on him about the ins and outs of the game.

Banks promised Serve that once he got out, if the game chose him, he would shoot Serve payment for the game he was blessing him with.

After they finished their meals, they headed to the bean slot so they could dump their trays. As they approached, Officer Jones slipped Banks a "kite" and whispered, "Read it when you get back to your cell."

Banks nodded, but he had to make a call first. He coolly told her, "I'll check it out and I'll get back to you."

She snickered and left the cell block.

Banks went to the phones on the wall and called Chrissy.

"Hello?" Chrissy sounded agitated.

"You have a collect call from..."

"It's me...Pick up."

"If you want to accept this call, press '0'."

After pressing 0, she could hear a lot of noise in the background. She could also hear that unmistakable voice that seemed to always get her kitty wet.

"Hello," Banks said.

"Hey, boo...How you holding up?" Chrissy sounded a lot more excited than she did when she answered the phone.

The thought made him smile. "What's the word? Did Killa already take the bread to Joe?"

Chrissy inhaled deeply and proceeded to tell Banks everything that had transpired. Banks couldn't believe what he was hearing. Then, to hear that his best friend and right-hand man was killed, that sent him over the edge. *What the fuck? I've been good to the game*, Banks thought bitterly.

"Baby...What should I do," Chrissy asked, hoping that he had some type of direction.

Banks' mind was so entangled that he couldn't think straight. He was speechless. "Look, babe...Um...Let me call you back. I need to, umm...Figure this shit out," Banks said. Without waiting for a response, he hung the phone up and stood there, trying to get his thoughts together. All he heard was white noise as heat tried to tear its way through his chest.

No money meant no freedom. "Fuck," he yelled in frustration. There was no way he'd be able to deal with them niggas in the day room, so instead, he walked back to his cell. After laying in the bunk for about an hour, he remembered he had the kite from Officer Jones in his pocket. He pulled it out and began to read.

"I know I'm taking a real big risk writing this down, but honestly I feel I can trust you. Since you've been on this tank, I've watched you and I'm impressed with your code of conduct. I looked you up and noticed you have a murder case. Look, I don't know if you have a girl, but I'm a woman who could play her position. I hate drama, but behind mine I'm willing to go the distance. I realize that you may already have something going on, so I'm willing to share. Ever since I laid eyes on you, I've wanted you. If you need anything, let me know. Oh, and please. flush this kite when you're done or give it back to me. PS... Call me Tracy."

Banks read the note 3 more times. He couldn't help but smile. *The game god had finally realized he fucked over a real nigga!* After calling Serve to his cell, he told him everything and they devised a plan. He wrote Tracy a response.

"Wassup, sexy? I really appreciate your words. Believe it or not, right now they're exactly what I needed to hear. To answer your question, yes, I do have a woman, but if you're willing to play your position, then we can definitely make something shake. You said I could ask if I needed something. Well, I have a proposition that could benefit the both of us..."

He went on to explain the different contrabands and what they were worth. He told her what he would pay for each trip and what type of security and protection he would offer her.

The day room phones were monitored, so the first thing he needed was a cell phone. When he was done writing, he came out of the cell and motioned for her to open the sally port doors. He came out and dropped the kite in the picket's bean shoot.

As he made his way back into the wing, she ran down the stairs and grabbed the kite. She read it, smiled and nodded. Now, all Banks had to do was wait for her to bring the phone so he could run everything down to her properly.

It's been 3 days since Chrissy told Banks the bad news. It's also been 3 days that went by with no visits. She couldn't bring herself to look him in the eye, knowing she couldn't do anything to help. She felt like she failed him. Like she was useless. Every time she talked to him on the phone, it felt like her heart was being ripped out of her chest. The last conversation ended with them arguing. She suggested that she get a job. Him telling her, "For what...? Whatever you make on a job won't put a dent in a 175K ticket!"

She cried her eyes out once she got off the phone. She felt so ashamed. She couldn't even do for herself, much less her man. The same man that had done so much for her the last 6 years. So far, all she'd been able to do was put $3,000 on his books. At least he wouldn't be hungry anytime soon. She sent him 200 pictures, but she knew that wasn't shit compared to regaining his freedom.

One thing she knew for sure. She needed a job. Even if Banks felt like he didn't need her money, she did. She hadn't had to work, thanks to him, but now that he's gone, it's grind time!

The only question is... Where? She scrolled through her call log and when she saw Tuck's number, her eyes lit up. *Of course. I know Tuck will know somebody that could give me a job.* She dialed his number.

"Hello?"

"Heyyy, Tuck," Chrissy sang out

"What's going on, baby girl? To what do I owe the pleasure? Don't tell me you want seconds," he said cockily.

"You got jokes, huh? Naw, Tuck, what I need is a job. Do you know anyone that would hire me?"

"Shit. Do you have any bartending experience," he asked.

Chrissy thought to lie, but for what? He would find out the truth the first day she worked. "No, I don't," she admitted, feeling sort of defeated.

"Well, look...I got a spot open. I've only got one bartender at night. Her name is Poptart. She can give you on-the-job training. I'll push for you to get your license, but until then, I'll pay you under the table."

Chrissy blew out a sigh of relief. She couldn't thank Tuck enough. Before she hung up, she asked, "When can I start?"

"No time like the present. Be here at 7. That way you can get a few hours of training before the doors open up."

"Bet! I'll be there." *I guess it is true what they say. It's not what you know, but who you know,* she thought as she realized this was her first smile since Banks went to jail. She was determined to find a way to get him out. She just didn't know how yet.

She looked at her diamond studded Rolex Banks had gotten for her last birthday. It was a quarter 'til 2. She had less than 5 hours to burn before she had to be at the club.

She decided to spend a little bit of the rainy-day funds. After all, she had to make a good first impression. She only had $4,000 dollars left but knew she'd be making money later that night. How much was yet to be seen. She grabbed her keys and headed to the Galleria.

Later that night, she pulled her pearl white BMW 650 into a deserted parking lot. *This bitch looks a whole lot bigger at night when the parking lot is packed,* she thought. She pulled her cell phone out and called Tuck. "I'm outside," she said as soon as he answered.

"Well, bring your fine ass inside," he said as he belted out a deep laugh.

Chrissy was so accustomed to calling him to escort her into the club that it never occurred to her to just walk in. As she entered the front door, she noticed Tuck's gigantic frame standing next to the bar. Instantly, flashbacks of his face wedged between her thighs, feasting on her goodies popped up in her head.

She felt her clit twitch as she leaned in to hug him and got a whiff of his Gucci cologne. "Hey, Tuck," she cooed as he made it a point to grab two handfuls of her big ole juicy booty.

"Damn, Chrissy...You sure know how to do it to a nigga... Don't you?"

"Boy... I don't know what you're talking 'bout. What am I supposed to be doing?" Chrissy smiles knowingly as she turns around to survey the club, at the same time giving Tuck a 360-degree view of her onion booty. She couldn't resist making it jump as she walked to the other side of the bar.

"Let me give you the tour," Tuck said as he began to walk her around the club. He took her to the VIP lounge, the restrooms, utility closet and every other square inch of the place. When he brought her back to her workstation, Poptart had returned from the restroom and had begun setting up. Tuck took the time to introduce them. "Poptart... This is our new bartender Chrissy...Chrissy, this is the longest tenured employee at the club. She's been here since it opened, so there's nothing she doesn't know how to do."

Poptart was what black men called a phenomenon. A white woman with an ass like a Kentucky thoroughbred Triple Crown winner. Standing at 5'4", green eyes with small, perky B cup titties, she was killing most sisters in the ass department. To top it off, she had fire red hair and matching freckles. She reminded you of Lindsey Lohan... The Straight Stunna version. Poptart smiled. "Hey. Tuck said you've never been a bartender before." It was a question, but sounded more like an accusation.

"Naw, I haven't," Chrissy admitted.

"Well, it's really not as difficult as people think. It's honestly all about memory glands." Chrissy just looked at her, unsure of what to say. Poptart continued. "Aight. I'm going to teach you the clubs 10 most popular drinks. If they order a drink that's not on the list, just tap my shoulder and I'll make it for you."

Chrissy felt so relieved. For the next 2 and a half hours, Poptart showed her how to mix the most requested drinks. When the club opened its doors at 10, she was confident she would do well. She was wrong!

The night started out okay, but once the volume of patrons increased, things got out of hand. People started complaining that she was moving too slow and that she was messing up the orders. One customer even had the nerve to throw a drink in her face, because he said he wanted Ciroc and not Grey Goose. Of course, he was promptly beaten down by two of the biggest bouncers in the club. All night long, dudes were coming on to her. She politely turned them down.

Once the night was over, she counted her tips and was highly disappointed. *A hundred and twenty fucking dollars. What the fuck? This ain't gone get a bitch anywhere, but in debt!* She almost broke down in tears as she brought Tuck the contents of the cash register.

When Tuck saw her face, he couldn't help but to ask, "What's wrong, C?"

"Mannn...Tuck, I thought I was going to make some money tonight. I went through hell out there, and I only brought in a 120 measly dollars!" Tuck couldn't help but chuckle to himself.

"C, it's your first night. Really, you did good out there for someone with no experience. Once you learn the drinks, your time will increase and so will your tips," Tuck preached. An image of Banks popped in her head, and a tear rolled down her cheek. "Something else is bothering you. Now, what's really good, baby doll?"

She debated whether or not she should tell him about her situation. Finally, she said fuck it and spilled her heart out. She told him everything from the robbery to Banks lawyer fees, to her feeling helpless. Tuck listened attentively. When she was finished, he stared at her for half a minute, then asked if she needed money. She looked at him through her red-stained eyes and gave him a solemn head nod.

Tuck breathed in deeply and told her, "Look...I can't give you no hundred plus bands, but I told you if you needed some more cash, don't hesitate to pull up on me."

"At what cost?" Chrissy sniffled.

"Well..." Big Tuck gets up and locks his office door.

Chrissy's really not in the mood for this, but what can she do? She *needs* the money. Especially after what she just made bartending.

Tuck walks up to her; the huge bulge in his slacks causing her pussy to tingle. He unzips his fly and tells her, "Get it out yourself! I want to see if you can make me cum in less than 3 minutes. If you can, I'll give you $5,000." He looks at his Hublot as Chrissy digs in his boxers and pulls out what has to be 9 inches of dick, still flaccid!

She never had to handle something so big, but for 5 bands, she'll break her neck trying...Literally!

"Go," Tuck shouts.

Chrissy dives in headfirst. Ferociously, she sucks on his plum-size head while massaging his nut sack with her right hand. Her left hand violently stroking his shaft, coaxing the nut from deep within his scrotum. She bobs her head as if her life depended on it.

"Fuck! Shit, girl.. Suck that dick," Tuck urges as Chrissy attempts a suicide mission.

She attempts to deep-throat his whole 11-inch girth. Only 3/4 is buried. She could feel his cock pulsate against her larynx.

"Yesss, that's it.. Swallow all that cock...Eat that dick, you nasty bitch."

Chrissy pulls it out, spits on it, then stuffs it back in her mouth. All in one fluid motion. Just sucking his dick has her feeling hot. She could feel her panties sticking to her pussy lips. Now that she's tasted cock, she fiends to have him knock the lining out her pussy! She knows time is ticking.

She turns it up a notch and goes into beast mode. Desperation takes over and she tries her luck. She reaches under his heavy nut sack and with an index finger, finds his backdoor.

"Oohh fuck... Whooooah...Don't stop!" *Bingo!*

Before she knew it, his nuts swelled up and his whole body became tense. With a quick jerk, hot nut shoots down her throat, coating her trachea. It's so much she couldn't possibly swallow it all. Some dribbled down her chin and stained her blouse.

Tuck looked at his watch. "2 minutes and 48 seconds... Damn, C! Girl, that was the best head I ever had!"

"What? You through," Chrissy challenged. Her pussy was dripping something serious and her mouth was slick with spit and cum. She needed her box pounded out.

"Hell mo!" Tuck eagerly replied.

"Good... 'Cause I need to have that big motherfucka split me in half." She grabbed a hold of his dick, licked the rest of the cum off the head and went back to work.

Once she had him back in working condition, she bent over his dick, ass tooted up in the air. Big Tuck pulled her thong down to her knees, grabbed a hold of his dick and slid deep off into her snatch.

"Ohhhh. Myyy. Fuucccckkkiiinnnnngg. Gawwwwdddd!" Chrissy never experienced anything like that. She felt him all the way in her throat. She reached back and realized he only had half his log up in her. "Hold up! Hold up! Hold up," Chrissy begged as she struggle to get adjusted.

Once she felt comfortable, Tuck went to work on her pussy. He fucked Chrissy 8 ways 'til Sunday. She had never felt so full in her life. Tuck knew just how to work his huge piece of equipment. When they were done, Chrissy was $5,000 richer and 3 orgasms lighter.

The next morning, as she slept like a baby, her phone rang. She fumbled to pick it up. "Hello?"

"You have a collect call fro..."

Click! She hung up the phone. She was just too tired to talk. *He'll call back later. I need some more sleep,* she told herself as she put her phone on vibrate and drifted back to sleep. Meanwhile, Banks continued to blow her phone up.

Chapter 7

Slam! Banks slammed the phone down once again. The whole day room looked in his direction, but once they noticed the stone-cold look of rage on his face, they went back to minding their own business. He'd called Chrissy at least 30 times in the last hour, and she hadn't picked up at all. *Dirty bitch. I bet she's the one that set me up,* he started to reason. Why else would she ignore his calls? He really wished his ace was still alive. Ever since he found out about Killa getting killed, every cat that came in the tank claiming he was from the South side, Banks made it his business to beat them down. So far, he was 3-0. He had to admit, he damn near lost the last one. If it wasn't for the nigga slipping, and Banks catching him with a right hook that put him to sleep, he might have gotten the short end of the stick.

Serve approached him as he sat watching TV. "Say, young playa. What's da bidness for the day?"

"Man, Unc, that no good bitch must have made a move. I ain't been locked up 2 months yet, and she's already on some fuck shit."

Serve takes his time to survey the situation before he speaks on it. "Well...Look at it this way. Now you have the time and energy to devote to breaking that lil' tender Tracy."

"That's another thing, Unc. It's been 2 weeks since I gave her the kite. She still ain't brought a nigga that jag yet," Banks said pointedly.

"Give her some time, nephew. She has to make sure that everything is done right. You know it's a felony if she gets caught, so have some patience, young brother. Remember, this game is played with patience and poise," Serve schooled.

"Chow time! Chow time! Everybody line up and get your trays."

As they line up, Officer Jones avoids eye contact with Banks and he finds that very suspicious but doesn't call her on it. When he grabs his tray, she slips a note between the slices of bread. He retrieved it, gave the tray away and rushed to his cell. He opened the note, read it and couldn't help but to smile.

"Hey, baby. I got that for you. What we can do is this. Right before rack time, come get the mop and broom. It will be in there. I already activated it. My number is programmed into the phone. When I get home, I need to hear your sexy ass voice."

Banks wanted to jump for joy. Later that night, he called her up to discuss everything he had planned. From packaging, to drop times, what to do if she ever got questioned. He assured her that he would fall before she ever would.

They talked until 3 in the morning. He explained that all the money he made, he would send to her. He would just have to trust that she would save it to pay the lawyer.

The only other piece to the puzzle was that she didn't have any drug connections. Banks didn't want her out there messing with anybody, so he hooked her up with his plug...Raul!

Next day, she brought 2 ounces of cocaine stuffed inside 2 condoms. She had shaped it to look like a dildo. It was nothing to slide up in her and walk through the checkpoint.

In jail, everything is exponential. In the streets, grams go for $50 to $80 apiece. In jail, $100 to $150. Multiply that by 28 and you're looking at $2,500 to $3,000 per zip, easy. With two of them, that's 5 bands on the first trip. Do that 2 or 3 times a week, a nigga will be out in no time. Then, heroin prices are even higher. The way Banks planned it, she would bring 2 ounces of coke, 2 ounces of Boy and 2 ounces of Ice every other week.

Banks never sold anything himself. He had a couple niggas from the world who were Bankroll Mafia. They were facing serious charges and needed as much help as they could. He would send them the work and they would be responsible for sending him the money.

For the most part, everything was going smoothly until this hardheaded lil' nigga by the name of Bishop tried to play Banks for soft. He swore up and down that he sent Tracy the money, but Tracy assured Banks that he never did. Banks even asked him for a screen shot as proof, but Bishop would always have an excuse as to why he couldn't send it yet. Banks shot word to Bishop that he had 24 hours to send the bread. Time came and went. Still, nothing.

Bishop was housed on the other side of the jail and felt as if he was untouchable. One day, Bishop got a lay-in to go to see medical that he didn't put in. He was under chronic care for his blood pressure, so he didn't think anything of it.

When they placed him in the holding cell, he didn't take notice that it was already occupied by 5 other individuals. He found an empty seat and waited to be called. Just as he was closing his eyes for a quick nap...*WHAP!* Blood flew from his mouth as he fell face first onto the cement bench. Next thing he knew, he was getting kicked in the ribs, kicked in the head and he knew for a fact he lost 3 teeth. Blood flooded his eyes. Blind and in excruciating pain, he didn't think the pain would ever cease. Finally, he lost consciousness.

When the officer finally came, Bishop was lying in a pool of blood, badly beaten but still breathing. He was life flighted. They locked up everyone that was present in that holding cell. Investigation took place. No one folded. After

30 days, they dropped it and allowed everyone to return to their housing assignments. As Banks finally walked into his old tank, he was heralded like a hero. While he was gone, Tracy continued to make drops to Serve. Serve made sure the money got to where it was supposed to.

Four and a half months later and going on 6 months since Banks had been locked up, he calculated that he should have close to 50K put up. Of course, he spent some on Tracy because she had deserved it. For the most part, he saved every dime he made.

One night, while they were on the phone, Tracy asked, "So, wassup? When you come home, you're moving in with me, right?" She had been pushing the subject for a minute, but Banks wasn't receptive to it. It wasn't that he didn't want to. He just wanted to give pimping a try. Something was telling him that he would be really great at it.

Serve had blessed him with some top-shelf game and he couldn't wait to get out there and go use it. He felt she would only get hurt in the process, and he didn't want to hurt her.

"Look, Tracy, I told you...I'm not sure about that. I mean, a nigga wants to. But I got to mash for that paper. I lost my whole life savings. Baby, I just don't want to hurt you," Banks said sincerely.

"Nigga... You act like I don't know 'bout the hustle," she replied. "My brothers, dad, uncles are all street niggas. I know what the streets are about."

Banks still hadn't told Tracy that he planned on pimping, and selling dope was a thing of the past. He honestly felt like if he told her now, she may quit on him. That's what worried him the most. He was almost at his goal and he couldn't afford to fuck it up with the truth. He made a promise to himself. When he reached the goal, he would tell her the plans for the future.

"How 'bout this, baby? I promise to move in with you, if you promise me you won't trip about the way I make my money, or if I'm sometimes gone."

"How long are you talking 'bout being gone, Brandon?"
"I really don't know. Maybe days at a time. Maybe a week here or a week there," he informed her.

"Well, I can deal with that if you put me first... And that means before the game, nigga," she tells him.

"Bet!" Banks agreed. After they had phone sex, he told her he loved her and hung up. He shot word to his stash man to come grab the phone so he could get some sleep. That night, he dreamt about copping 3 bad snow bunnies and coming down in a Bentley with gators, minks and six figures worth of jewelry. For some reason, he dreamt of Tracy and Chrissy side by side. 2 of his best hoes. Oh well, a nigga can dream can't he?

It's been 6 months since she'd talked to Banks. He hadn't called and she hadn't had time to go visit. She'd been working herself dog tired at the club and usually didn't get home until 6 in the morning. By the time she gets her 6 to 8 hours in, get up, do her hygiene and shop, she doesn't have time for anything else but to go to work. She attempted to write a few times, but he never responded to her letters. *I know he thinks I left him in there stranded. Little does he know, I'm out here stacking for him.*

In 6 months, Chrissy was able to stack up $25,000. That may not seem like a lot to some, but considering her habits, that was pretty damn good. She still remembered the night she stumbled upon her master plan.

She was working the bar on a Wednesday night which happened to be one of the few nights the club wasn't jammed packed. An older white gentleman approached the bar and took a seat. Even though Club Heat was known for having a diverse crowd, it was still a surprise to see an older white man patron the night club. She immediately gave him a quick assessment and categorized him as a great tipper dressed in a black and gold Versace dress shirt with black slacks, Valentino slip-ons and a yellow gold Patek Philippe.

Chrissy couldn't deny it. Even though she wasn't traditionally into white men, dude was sexy as hell. Salt and pepper hair, piercing blue eyes. Even though she could tell he had to be in his late 40's, early 50's, he had the physique of a 30-year-old athlete.

"What's your sin tonight, sir," she inquired as she prepared to fill his order.

The older gentleman smiled, and Chrissy's pulse skipped and trotted. "Please... Call me David," he replied. "And my sin tonight will be a... White Russian."

While mixing the drink, Chrissy could feel his ice blue eyes burning a hole through the side of her head. It didn't make her feel uncomfortable. Actually, her pussy began to come alive.

When she placed his drink in front of him, his eyes peered into her soul. "So, what's your name," he asked as he ran his finger around the rim off his glass.

"Sunshine," Chrissy claimed. She learned early on from Poptart that she needed an alias.

"Because these fools get crazy sometimes," she told Chrissy one night.

"Crazy like... Stalk and try and rape a bitch crazy?" Chrissy hadn't even fathomed that something like that could happen.

She hears David speak, and it brings her back to the present. "Well, Sunshine...You are a very extravagant and beautiful woman. I would love to do nothing but sit here and gaze at you all night."

"Umm...Ooookkaaaayy." Chrissy couldn't hide her blush. He tipped her $50 which was twice what his drink cost. She politely thanked him and went back to serving other customers.

As the night went on, there were many more admirers, but David remained a staple in her mind. Probably because he sat rooted in his seat. Doing exactly what he said he'd be doing. Gazing at her.

Half an hour before closing time, he made his move. "Sunshine. I would like to ask you a question, but I don't want you to feel insulted."

"Okay...Wassup," Chrissy asked suspiciously.

"Well, I'm a man who enjoys a woman's company and I don't mind compensating them for their time. I've been watching you all night, and I would want nothing more than to enjoy *your* company for the rest of the evening."

She took a few seconds to contemplate his offer. "How much," she finally asked.

"I'll give you a thousand for each hole you let me penetrate," he propositioned.

Chrissy felt a spurt of her juices wet the crotch of her panties. "$3,000 it is then," she confirmed with a seductive smile.

After she left work, she followed him to Hotel Derek off 6-10 and Westheimer. David purchased a Presidential suite, then they made their way to the elevator. As they entered the room, Chrissy told him she needed to shower first. He also needed one, but they decided to take theirs separately. Once both were thoroughly clean, David laid her down on the king-size bed. He began to suck on her meaty pussy lips. He slid his thumb inside her box and massaged the thin layer between her asshole and her pussy. Before she knew it, Chrissy was squirting all over his chin.

She bucked against his hand, begging. "Ohh, shit! Fuck me, please, David. Let me see what that dick feels like."

David stood up and for the first time she got a good look at his fully erect member. She was pleasantly surprised. It was about 8 inches. Long, thick and hearty. *Hopefully he knows how to work it,* she thought. He strapped the condom on and dove between her folds.

The white man definitely didn't disappoint. With stroke after delicious stroke, David fucked her with patience and precision. He sexed her so good that even after the fact, she could still feel her walls vibrating from the beat down he gave. She hadn't had dick so precise since Banks went to jail. Tuck made her cum, but his dick was too big to enjoy completely. She began to just give him head for the bread.

When she woke up the next morning, David was gone. She found $4,000 on the nightstand, with a note.

"I had a beautiful night. I hope you enjoyed it as much as I did. Here goes the $3,000 we agreed upon as well as an extra $1,000 for taking it all without complaint. Whenever you're up for another round call 832..."

"Damn!" she said out loud to herself. "That man fucked me silly. I don't even know where my cell phone is." After a brief search, she found it and logged his number in. She went ahead and texted him so he could log hers.

Chrissy: Say David. This is Sunshine. Make sure you save my number.

Moments later, he texts back.

David: Perfect

Since then, he utilized her services a few more times. Once, he even brought a friend along. Of course he paid double the rate, but now she had begun to use her job as a spot to meet and greet before she decided if she wanted to deal with a client.

Things were starting to look up for her. She was busy at work, waiting on one of her newest clients named Charles. As he walked in, Chrissy lost her breath. Standing before her was a monster of a man. Standing at 6'7" 290-pounds, skin black as tar, Charles was a very imposing figure. She felt a serious case of unease but chalked it up to his stature. Charles was even *bigger* than Big Tuck. She made a note of his beady eyes. They kept darting back and forth as if he was high off something.

He approached the bar, sat down and introduced himself. "Sunshine, how are you doing?"

"Uhh...Charles, right," Chrissy asked, somewhat wishing she had the wrong guy.

"Yup. In the flesh. Frank told me I wouldn't be disappointed. So far, I'm definitely not," he said while he ogled her breast.

Chrissy was used to dudes leering at her. Sometimes, she even welcomed it, but something about Charles just didn't sit right. "Yeah? Well, Frank told me that you and him were close. I've been dealing with Frank for some months now, so I'ma take his word for it," Chrissy told him.

After they made small talk and against her better judgment, she agreed to leave with him and get a room. Of course, she'd be following him in her car.

As they exited the club, Chrissy noticed all four of her tires were slashed. "Ughh...What the fuck!" She tried to think of anyone that would have a motive to do something like that to her, but her mind drew a blank. Honestly, it could have been anyone. A disgruntled customer or a hating ass coworker who felt slighted about something trivial. She made a mental note to have Tuck check the security cameras when she got to work the next day. Chrissy slapped the hood of the car in frustration and felt a heavy presence behind her.

"You can just ride with me and I'll bring you back in the morning," Charles suggested.

As a rule, Chrissy knew to never find herself in a situation where she couldn't come and go as she pleased. Yet and still, her greed took over. Her better judgment screamed, "No!" but she pushed it to the side and hopped into his all-black SUV.

"You want something to eat before we head out," he asked as they were pulling out of the club's parking lot.

"Umm...Yeah, we can go ahead and stop at a fast-food spot real quick," she suggested.

They pulled up through the drive-thru and ordered their meals. As they were leaving, Charles patted his pockets and said, "Damn! I forgot to get some condoms."

"Well, pull up to the gas station. I'll run in and get them. I need to grab a few things anyway... What kind?"

"Magnums," Charles claimed.

Chrissy smirked as she thought, *Yeah, everybody's Willy Wonka with the golden ticket these days.* "I just hope you can fit them," she mumbled to herself as she stepped out of the vehicle. 10 minutes later, she returned and they were headed to the room... Or maybe they weren't. "Where we gong? You just passed up 2 different motels," Chrissy asked as she sipped on her soft drink.

"I got a crib not too far from here. We'll just crash there tonight," Charles told her with ice dripping off his words.

He must be a cheap motherfucka... Trynna skip out of paying for a room, she thought.

She took another sip from her drink. Her eyelids began to feel heavy. *Something's wrong!* She immediately starts to panic. Her heartrate triples up. She hears it beating loudly in her eardrums. She couldn't breathe. Her limbs felt like jelly. The last thing she remembered was Charles staring at her with those same beady eyes. Then everything went black!

When Chrissy finally awoke, she found herself laying in a bathtub. She noticed a faint smell of bleach. Charles sat on the edge of the tub, giving her a sponge bath. She felt a sharp ache between her legs and tried to formulate the words to ask what happened, but her tongue felt like lead. She blacked out once again.

"Bitch! Wake up." *SMACK!* "Wake your ass up!"

Chrissy's eyes shot open. Her face felt like it was on fire. She didn't know where she was exactly, but something told her she needed to be thankful she was still alive.

"Get out...And bitch, if you tell anybody about this...You're dead! You understand?"

She couldn't do anything but nod. She struggled to open the door, obviously still weak from the ordeal.

Charles, tired of her feeble attempts, reached across her, grabbed the handle and forced the door open. Chrissy wasn't fully out of the vehicle when Charles hit the gas, leaving her stranded in a strange hood, in the middle of the night.

As her wits returned and the effects of the drug wore off, the ache between her legs became a crippling pain. She came to the heartbreaking realization. *That motherfucka raped me!* Tears began to cascade down her cheeks. She frantically wiped them away.

With no phone, no money, she needed to find out where she was so she could make her way back home. She took off walking, noting the predatorial stares from the hustlers on the corners. She could only imagine what she must look like walking down the street in a skirt, barefoot.

"Who is this thick, yellow bone chick who just mysteriously dropped out of the sky," a worn and battered dope fiend named Sheryl asked her imaginary friend. She approached Chrissy unafraid. "Do you have a dollar?"

Chrissy held out her hands, palms up, signifying she didn't have anything. "I don't even have a dollar to my name," she told the crackhead. The woman shrugged her shoulders and made a move to leave. Chrissy stopped her. "Can you please tell me where I'm at?"

The old woman smiled, showing her vacant gums. "Honey...You in the Tre!"

Aww shit...The Southside...Third Ward! She watched as the woman took off back down the street. Chrissy felt helpless. Scared to death. Not because she was in an unfamiliar neighborhood at 4 in the morning, half dressed, walking barefoot, but because she didn't know what Charles had done to her. Her whole body felt sore. Her asshole felt as if it was bleeding. Tears began to fall, but she quickly wiped them away.

She could hear a Bass system bumping as a black Monte Carlo on Swangas pulled up next to her. Sitting inside were two males, both in their early twenties. The driver was brown skinned, taper fade with a mouth full of invisible set diamonds. No doubt, he got them done by TV Johnny. The passenger was of a darker complexion. He wore his hair in the gumby ramp. His grill had blue sapphires.

"Wassup, lil' momma? Where you from," the driver asked.

She had originally told herself that she wouldn't talk to them, but her common sense and survival instinct took over. She was on foot and they were in a car, so at the end of the day, she needed to play nice so she could find a way home. She stopped, turned towards the car and addressed the driver. "I'm from the East and I'm trynna get back home."

"The East?" The passenger sat up in his seat. "What part of the East?"

Chrissy figured out her mistake, but it was too late. She had totally forgotten. The South and the East were going to war behind what happened to Killa. She thought about Banks and her heart ached. She really wished he was home. What she was going through would have never happened. "I'm from Coolwood," she lied. She could assess that they were Crips, and telling them she was from Hunterwood was not about to help her cause. She chose one of the most crip'd out hoods on the East to claim.

"Oh yeah? Do you know the homie J Bang," the passenger asked. Chrissy never ventured to Coolwood, so she didn't know anyone from there. Well, except one.

"Naw. I don't know J Bang, but I do know Paccy," she revealed.

The driver's eyes lit up. "Oh shit. You know OG Paccy," he asked in disbelief as if she just said Denzel or Obama.

"Yeah, we used to fuck around," she half lied.

The driver looked at her in a new light. If OG Paccy was fucking her, she must have some good pussy. "Okay. Well, check game. I'll give you a ride, but I need some gas money," the driver said, knowing she was broke at the moment.

"I don't have any money."

"Well, if you let a nigga sample them goods, I'll drop you off anywhere you need to go," the driver said while licking his lips suggestively.

I can't believe this shit, Chrissy thought as she weighed her options. "Look. I'm on my period. I'll give you some head to take me home."

"*Us,*" the passenger added.

Chrissy looked at the driver. He just shrugged his shoulders. "Uggghhh," she groaned with frustration as she climbed into the backseat with the passenger first.

After they took turns fucking, then cumming in her mouth, they dropped her off on Federal Road. She couldn't afford to let them know she stayed in Hunterwood. She began the 3 mile walk home. She wasn't worried though. The East belonged to her man, and she belonged to him. The respect was always evident. When she got home, she took a hot, scalding bath. With a glass of Hennessy to the head, she cried until she drifted asleep.

Chapter 8

The after-hour spot was packed. Paccy and all his Insane G's were up in the place celebrating, like they'd just won the Super Bowl. A little while back, Paccy had stumbled upon a sweet lick, and they hadn't looked back ever since. Paccy had found them an out-of-town plug. His young niggas were moving heavy meth and soft in the city.

His $1,200 Robin jeans sagged just a little. Champagne spilled all over his all-black Balenciaga sneakers. No shirt on. Tattoos on full display. You couldn't tell him anything. *Who would have thought,* he told himself as he hoisted up a bottle of Ace of Spades. "Insane Guerilla Family," he shouted as his crew began to beat on their chest in unison.

Dorian watched the display in awe. It seemed Paccy had come up faster than a dick on Viagra. He always had some change to play with, but now it seemed like he could legitimately make the claim as "The Man in The City!" She had been invited to the after party by one of Paccy's close lieutenants. A killer by the name of Dread.

Now Dread was 6'4", slim, but carried a very big and heavy gun. A gun that he definitely enjoyed using. He made average money, but his money wasn't what she was in love with. It was dick! She simply couldn't get enough of it. Every chance she got it, she sucked, fucked and nutted on his cock. Tonight, she planned on seeing if she could fuck some intel out of Dread about Paccy. Dread received a text message.

"I'll be right back," he told her as he got up and headed to the men's restroom.

Dorian waited and waited. She saw different faces enter and leave the restroom, but no sign of Dread. *Damn...This nigga been in there for the last 18 minutes,* she thought. She contemplated going in there but thought better of it. No doubt, he would be pissed. With all those different men with their dicks out, knowing her, she would get caught looking.

"Damn, baby girl! You thick as hell," a deep voice reverberated in her ear. She turned to see OG Paccy himself. Standing at 6'2", onyx black skin, he towered over her, but she didn't feel fear. What she felt was...Intrigue. She stared deep off into his eyes. "What's your name?"

Dorian thought about lying for the sake of Dread but said to hell with it. "Dorian...But people call me D Money!"

"D Money, huh? I like that. So, who you here with?" It was obvious he was pissy drunk, but he was handling it very well.

She looked at the bathroom door once again and said, "No one."

"Well… In that case, I'm trynna dip outta here. You riding?"

Damn… I might not get another chance to find out what's going on with this nigga. If Dread finds out though...

Sensing her hesitation, Paccy sucked on her right earlobe and whispered, "I wanna suck on this pussy all night long 'til you drown me in cum."

Goddamn, she thought. There was no way she was about to pass that invitation up. With a soft moan escaping her lips, she nodded and said, "Let's go!" If she would have waited 10 more seconds, she would have seen Dread coming out of the restroom, followed by a chick from her hood named Candace.

Half drunk and staggering, Candace came out with her skirt flipped up, exposing her freshly fucked cunt. She turned around and spoke to someone, and as soon as she turned back around, Dread was gone. She was left standing alone. She hung her head in shame. *I can't believe I let them niggas run a train on me,* she thought. *All in the name of love.*

Shlurp...Shlurp...Shlluuuuurrrppp! Dorian sucked on his dick like an everlasting fortune was buried in his nut sack.

"Ohh shit! Suck that motherfucking dick, bitch! Fuuucckk!"

Dorian was happy to oblige. Cuffing his sack, she began massaging his balls. His nuts tightened and she knew he was mere seconds away from exploding. She craved to eat his cum. She grabbed the base of his dick, squeezed tightly as she sucked on the head.

Paccy began to tremble as his nuts boiled to a dangerous level, with no release. Just as he thought he was about to pass out, she released her grip and his cock exploded. Quarts of hot cum spattered her face, drenching her lips. With a loud smack, she cleaned his knob and squeezed out what was left.

"Damn!" Paccy could barely think straight. "That was the best head I ever had," he panted.

With a small chuckle, Dorian responded, "That's because I'm by far the baddest bitch you ever had!"

"I can't even dispute that. That was something else," he admitted. That was just the appetizer as they sat in his truck outside of his condo.

Once they got inside, they touched every room, every spot and performed every position. She wanted to lock Paccy down, so she pulled out every trick in her book. When the session was over, Paccy laid passed out while Dorian went through her voicemails. Dread left three different messages asking her where in the hell she was. *Too bad!*

Even though Dread had a longer dick, Paccy's money was longer. Add that to the fact that he could fuck and suck like a porn star. Game over! She kept cycling through her voicemails until she came across one where Chrissy was crying.

Dorian called her phone, but it went straight to voicemail. *What the fuck?* She tried again, same results. She hung up but told herself she would go by her house later that day.

She looked back at the bed. Paccy was sleeping peacefully. She was tempted to go in his pockets but decided to give him an early morning treat instead.

With his limp rod in her tiny hand, she blew on it then proceeded to give him some slow and methodical head. Good thing she thought twice about going in his pockets. Paccy had hidden cameras positioned all over the condo. He also learned from his last mistake with Chrissy. Unbeknownst to Dorian, two of his soldiers were posted in the parking lot with strict orders not to allow her to leave until he gave them the signal. If she would have tried to leave and catch a cab, she would have been beaten down before the cab arrived.

*** *

"Wakey! Wakey! Wakey!"

Banks opened his eyes and saw 4 country fed, white and black officers in his cell. One positioned near the toilet, just in case he tried to flush the contraband. *Fuck... Shakedown team,* he thought. He wondered who could have sent them his way. He knew eventually they would pull up to his door. Yet and still, no matter how much you're prepared, you still hate to see them.

"Get up and strip out."

"What's this all about, Ms. Piggy?" Banks knew he was clean, so he had a little room to talk a little shit. Every night before he went to sleep, he would send everything to the stash house. He knew that the shakedown team always hit early in the morning. He refused to let them catch him slipping.

After removing every article of clothing, spreading his ass cheeks, coughing as well as lifting up his nut sack, he was escorted to the captain's office.

As he entered, the leather faced captain, who was adequately named by inmates and officers as "Leather Face", was looking through several papers on his desk. Banks caught a 6x10 photo of Tracy. "Have a seat, Mr. Banks," the captain instructed.

After seating himself in the wooden chair with hand restraints on, Banks looked at the captain and asked, "What s this all about, Captain? I've been here going on a year, and I don't have any major or minor cases."

The captain looked at him for a bit before he decided to answer. "Well, Mr. Banks... This isn't about your disciplinary record. This is about your improper relationship with one of my female officers. The same one that's helping you run an elaborate drug operation in my jail." As if to punctuate his statement, Captain Garza slams his right hand onto the desk.

Failing to have the desired effect, Banks yawns as if he's tired of the spectacle and nonchalantly says, "Captain... I don't know what you're talking 'bout."

"Oh, you don't, huh?" He pulls out a stack of I-60's, or Snitch Reports. Each one detailing the relationship between Officer Tracy Jones and Inmate Brandon Banks. He feigned indifference, but truly was very attentive to what was being said. He wanted to see if they actually had enough to cost Tracy her job. *They don't have shit but a bunch of jailhouse snitches,* he surmised.

One thing he knew for sure... He was headed to lock up for 30 days, under investigation. He was more worried about Tracy. She was supposed to have brought him 2 ounces of Tar later that day. Hopefully Serve follows up with the plan. Banks always stressed, if anything happened to him, call Tracy ASAP and warn her not to come to work. To either call in, or make sure she didn't have anything on her.

After a few rounds of fruitless questioning, the captain ordered deputies to put him in one of the solitary cells for investigation. With no food, no correspondence, his first 12 hours were hell. He was sick with worry. Not knowing if his baby was alright or not.

"Chow time!" An SSI, or inmate janitor, brought the food around. Banks recognized him immediately. It was Doodie. One of his customers who stayed on the Trustee side of the jail. As he passed him his tray, Doodie whispered, "Under the patty."

Banks acknowledged him with a nod and replied, "'Preciate it, fam!"

"100," Doodie replied as he walked off to the next cell.

Banks lifted the meat patty and found the kite. It was from Serve.

"What's popping, young Playa? I heard what happened as soon as I got up. I took care of that. Your sister said hi. She told me to tell you she talked to the lawyer. She paid him what she had on deck and applied for a loan to cover the rest. She said to tell you she loves you and can't wait for you to come home. She'll write when she can."

Banks read the kite 3 more times and couldn't help but smile. He had some solid motherfuckers in his corner. Serve took care of the business, and Tracy stayed solid and followed instructions to the tee. He was hoping, with the loan, they would have enough.

One thing for sure, Banks wasn't going to have her bring in anything else. She was too valuable. She showed her worth and he didn't want to do anything that would risk losing her. He could almost smell the free world. He drifted off to sleep, and for the first time in a while, he slept peacefully.

***

Saturday night at the club was pure chaos. Legally, the club could only accommodate 1,200 people, but tonight? They had at least 2,000 bodies packed like sardines. The bar was jumping like Jordan. Chrissy and Poptart were working double-time trying to make sure everybody's orders were filled on time and correctly. The two women had gotten closer over the months.

That night, they had coordinated their outfits. Chrissy had on a red Marc Jacobs tube top with red pleated skirt and black Coach sneakers. Her hair was pulled back in a ponytail cascading down the middle of her back. Sweat had her baby hairs glistening. Poptart, on the other hand, was rocking a black Valentino top with a red Michael Kors skirt. To top it off, she had on red and black Versace sneakers. Her hair was done in Shirley Temple curls. Together, they had every man in the club buying drinks, just to get a shot at one, if not both of them.

Poptart looked at her G-Shock. It was almost 1:30AM. This was around the time when the bar started to slow down a bit. Everyone was drunk and now trying to secure someone to take home for the night.

As the traffic started to wind down, Chrissy took a moment to exhale. "Damn, girl! Tonight was hectic as hell," she told Poptart as she wiped the counter off.

"Yeah, but the tip jar looks healthy as hell, though!"

Chrissy glanced at the big juice jug they converted into a tip jar. By her estimates, they probably had $700 to $800 for the night. She forced a smile but couldn't help but miss her $3,000-$5,000 nights when she was turning tricks. Ever since that incident with Charles, she refused to turn another one. She was lucky she'd lived through the ordeal and didn't want to tempt lady luck again.

"Well, hold me down, girl... I'm 'bout to go use the little girls' room," Poptart said as she made her way to the restroom.

Chrissy watched her ghetto booty sway and switch, captivating every man and some women. As she got lost in her thoughts, she recognized a voice she knew to be familiar.

"Excuse me, sexy... Do you think I could bother you for a drink?" She turned and saw him for the first time in almost a year. Sitting there dressed to the nines— peach-colored Givenchy dress shirt with white slacks, white and gold Ferragamo slip-ons, and of course, no socks. He had on clear framed Fendi glasses with gold trim on the rims. Not to be outdone, his bling was immaculate. A Yatch Master Rolex with a bezel filled with VVS diamonds. His pinky ring set it off. It was yellow gold with white and pink diamonds. She estimated the ring to cost $15,000 by itself.

Damn...What was his name, she tried to remember. She had lost his card and hadn't seen him since. She had really, in all honesty, forgotten about him. But damn... He was looking sexy to her. "Uhh, sure... What's your sin," she stammered out.

"Well, I'm not a big drinker. How 'bout you give me something light? Something I know how to handle? How 'bout some... Pink Panties?" He looked at Chrissy's outfit and said, "Somehow, I doubt you're a woman who doesn't match her panties with her outfits."

Chrissy's face flushed. Mainly because she had on red and pink laced La Perla panties on. At that moment, they were sticking to her freshly waxed sex lips. Sensing her hesitation, he offered to accept whatever drink she suggested. "One Incredible Hulk coming right up." As she fixed his drink, she tried desperately to remember his name.

When Poptart returned, her green eyes lit up. "Heyyy, Saint," she screamed with delight. She ran over and gave Saint a great, big hug.

That's his name, Chrissy realized. *Saint Lucian!*

"Hey, P! Why you ain't tell me you had such a gorgeous coworker?"

"Well, maybe that's 'cause you're always out of town," she pouted.

"Uhh, here you go. One Incredible Hulk." Chrissy sat the drink down in front of him. Before she could remove her hand, his was on top of hers.

"Damn, girl...I never thought I'd see you again," he whispered in her ear.

She didn't know why, but Saint made her very nervous. "I was going through some shit, but I'm good now," she told him.

"In that case, take my card... *Again.* Use it this time." With that, Saint took his drink and told Poptart to call him when she got off work.

As soon as he left, Chrissy couldn't wait to get the scoop from her. "Sooo. How do you know Saint?" Chrissy bombarded her.

Poptart looked at her and laughed. "Girl... That's my big bro...Better yet, he's like my dad. He taught me a lot. I had run away from home when I was young. I ended up staying at a friend's house. Well, she stayed with her boyfriend Jason. One day, while she was at work, he and his homeboys were at the house smoking and playing on the game. Back then, I thought I could hang with the best of them. I smoked and drank 'til I passed out.

"Next thing I know, I wake up and Jason's fucking me from the back while his homeboy's rubbing his dick across my lips. The whole time their other homeboy's in the corner taping everything. I tried to stop them, but Jason said if I didn't cooperate, he would make sure I wouldn't have a place to stay. When it was all said and done, I was on camera getting trained on. Of course, I didn't tell my homegirl. When she found out, I was out on my ass. Imagine that!

"So... As I'm walking to nowhere in the middle of the night, an all-white Jaguar pulls up. Inside driving was the finest man I had ever laid eyes on. He asked if I needed a ride. I was hesitant, but I was so tired of walking. When I got in, he asked where I was going. I broke down, girl. I told that man everything. Since I didn't have anywhere to go, he took me to his house so I could eat, shower and get a good night's sleep. Oh, and before you ask...No, I didn't fuck him," she added, clearly reading Chrissy's mind. "But...We did end up getting close. We're like a team...Better yet, like family. I owe him my life!"

Chrissy did the math. They've been knowing each other for at least 5 years. "What does he do? Obviously, he's banked up," she asked curiously.

"Girl, just hit him up. He doesn't lie or sugarcoat. His motto is, *No lies, just loyalty!* If you ask, you shall receive. With that, Chrissy had made up her mind. Later that night, she hit Saint up.

They talked well into the night. When daylight peeked through the blinds, she still didn't want to get off the phone, but knew if she didn't, she'd be no good for work.

She asked if he'd be coming up to her job. He promptly told her no. "When you're getting to that bag, you need to be focused. I don't ever want to be the reason you lose focus. If anything, I'm trynna be the reason you *are* focused."

At the mention of money, Chrissy asked, "So what *do* you do for a living?"

"Well, I'm into management," he honestly replied.

"Oh, okay. So you manage entertainers? Like rappers and stuff," she asked, clearly intrigued.

"Yeah, I manage entertainers, but not rappers. My clients are adult entertainers."

Chrissy thought for a second. "You mean, like porn stars," she inquired.

"Well... Porn is one field, but they also dance, model... Really anything dealing with the sex industry."

"How much do they make?" Now Chrissy was extremely interested.

"Uhmm... I got girls on roster who make between $1,200 to $1,600 a night. Then, I have some that make $3,000 to

$5,000 a night? It's all on how you apply yourself," he schooled her.

"So, what's your percentage? What's your management fee?"

Saint never hesitated. "A hundred percent."

Silence engulfed the phone. Chrissy tried to digest all the information she just received. You could almost hear the gears turning in her brain. "So, you're a Pimp," she states more as an assessment than an accusation. She honestly didn't expect him to be truthful, but he surprised her.

After explaining what Pimping is truly about, he went on to give her some of the finer points to the game. When she wanted to know more, he informed her that "only those who choose will get the rules!"

By the time they finally did get off the phone, Chrissy was more than interested in the game. But could she be a nigga's hoe? She realized that she was already indulging in the game. With the right protection, guidance and security, she could definitely come up and get Banks out of jail. Then it hit her. How could she do that if Saint keeps all the money? If she decided to get under his pimping, she would need to come up with some type of way she could help Banks in the process. She went to sleep with it on her mind.

When she awoke, she called her best friend Dorian, hoping she could give her some sound advice. *Voicemail.* She decided to get her day started. Lately, she'd been talking less and less to Dorian. It seemed as though she'd been real standoffish with her. *Maybe it's because I've been working so much lately?* She chalked it up to that. She stripped out of her T-shirt and panties, and slid into the steaming hot bath. She began to daydream about Saint. Her hand slowly made its way to her coochie. With a few expert flicks of her clit, Chrissy came with an explosion. Her juices marinated into the bath water.

Of course, Dorian couldn't hear the phone ring when Chrissy called. She was too busy snorting coke off Paccy's big ass dick. She'd already snorted 3 lines and after 2 shots of Patron, was feeling no pain. After that very first night, her and Paccy had been inseparable. He'd ended up getting into it with his longtime girlfriend Tasha, and ended up spending his days shacked up with his new honey dip. He loved a freak and she *loved* being his sex slave. Of course, her services came with a fee, but Paccy was far from stingy.

Every time they had one of their wet and wild nights, he'd break her off a couple bands to do what she wanted with it. Add that to the fact they were fucking like jack rabbits, it didn't take a rocket scientist to see why Dorian didn't mind snorting a little coke. She even smoked wet with him once.

Her goal at first was to find out how Paccy got on. The rumor was he was the one that had gotten Banks. His crew was tight lipped about it. Either that, or they didn't know their damn selves.

As far as Paccy, the closest he got to revealing his come up was when he told one of his lieutenants, "Sometimes you gotta let your nuts hang and your gun bang in order to come up! I had to run up in a nigga shit to get what I got, but once I got it, I had to make it work for me!"

Dorian felt like he was talking about Banks, but she could never prove it. After a while, she stopped trying. The money, the dick, and not to mention the drugs, were a great distraction. After she thoroughly cleansed his dick of residue, his phone rang.

"Yo...? Oh, you 'bout to pull up...? Aight!"

I wonder who that is, Dorian asked herself. Just as the thought developed in her mind, there was a knock at the door.

"Can you get that for me," Paccy said as he got up and made his way into the kitchen to grab something.

She got up with nothing but a black Victoria Secret thong on. She threw on a silk robe and went to answer the door. The instant she opened the door, her heart dropped to her stomach.

Standing there with a menacing scowl on his face was none other than Dread. For the last couple weeks, she'd been giving him the run around and just straight up lying to him when he'd call trying to hook up.

"Let him in, D," Paccy called out as he was entering back into the living room.

"Yeah... Let me in, you filthy bitch," Dread gritted through his teeth.

This can't turn out good, Dorian thought as she stepped aside and allowed Dread to walk in the apartment. As he made his way in, Dread put on a smile to meet his Capo.

"What's crackin Cuz?"

They first locked up the C, then the IGF handshake. Paccy turned to Dorian and made the introductions. "Dorian, this my nigga Dread. He been wit me since day one. Dread...This my new wifey, D Money."

Dread smirked with his eyebrows raised. "Oh, shit... Wifey? I ain't know you stopped fucking wit Tasha!"

"Naw...I ain't left T. We just chilling right now," Paccy informed him. "D Money know what it is. She's keeping it all the way P for a nigga. Ain't that right, baby?"

Dorian had to clear the lump in her throat before she could answer. "Oh, yeah baby, you know I ain't doing no tripping." Dread shot daggers at her with his eyes. Chills ran through her bones. She knew then, it'd be only a matter of time before he came to kill her. Only solace she had was the fact that she was messing with Paccy, and Dread had a lot of respect for him. Hopefully, that would be enough for her to receive a pass. Just as she was starting to feel a little safe, Paccy got up and headed to the restroom.

"Aww, Cuz...Lemme find out, you can't handle yo' liquor. That Hen got you pissing like a racehorse," Dread said fishing.

"Naw, Cuz, it ain't the Hen. It's that white girl. Every time I fuck with that shit, a gangsta got to take a gangsta. I really need to lay off it," Paccy responded as he left the living room.

"Well, make 'sho yo' ass dump one, flush one, or at least take the air freshener," he shouted out jokingly. As soon as Paccy shut the bathroom door, Dread couldn't help but to smile. He knew he had a little time to work clean. Before she could blink, he shot off the couch like a panther, grabbing her by the throat. Through clenched teeth he told her, "Bitch! You think you gon' play me like some chump ass sucka? You think just cuz you wit da big homie you get a pass?"

"I was gonna tell you, Dread... I swear," she pleaded.

"Bitch! Shut the fuck up. I ain't trynna hear that shit. Matter fact, I got something that'll keep yo' mouth closed." He shoved Dorian on the ground, reached in his sweats and pulled out his python. "You better hurry up before he gets back," Dread warned.

Dorian knew if Paccy caught her in that compromising position, he would never believe that Dread made her do it. The only option was to finish him off before Paccy came out of the bathroom.

With one more glance at the bathroom door, she reached for his dick and shoved as much as she could down her wet throat. One hand caressing his balls, the other stroking his massive tool. Back and forth, up and down. Dorian sucked, slurped and swallowed. She bobbed on the dick with the skills of a seasoned porn star. Opening her throat to accommodate his massive size. She knew his cock like she knew the back of her hand. Within minutes, his balls tightened and his shaft pulsated.

"Agghh fuck... Shit! Here it comes, bitch!"

Spurts of warm dick milk splashed on her tongue, oozing down her throat. She wouldn't dare leave any evidence for Paccy to discover, so she swallowed every nut particle she could find.

"Oohh, shit! I see your nasty ass still got it," Dread huffed exhaustingly. He shook his dick over her face, allowing tiny droplets of cum to rain on her.

No sooner after they finished and had gotten up, the toilet flushed. They could hear Paccy washing his hands out in the sink. Dorian hurried up and ran to the bedroom to fetch her a bottle of mouthwash. There was no way she was about to talk to Paccy with dick on her breath. That'd be trifling! When she returned, Dread was on his way out the door. Her heart was pounding. She didn't know if Dread had given up her secret. She soon found out via a video message.

It was a video clip of Dorian going ham on Dread's dick. Swallowing everything he had to offer. *He must have taped it on his phone,* she admonished herself. The text read: *Bitch. When I call U cum. Or I lace my nigga up 'bout how dirty u r. He'll green light ure trash ass. Lol (laughing face emoji)* She wanted to cry. How the hell did she slip up like that, and let the nigga record her. She wanted to tell Paccy, but she knew he would take it the wrong way. Dread was his day one nigga, and she was just a piece of pussy. She already knew they lived by the code. *Bros before Hoes!* She had to think of something. And think of it quick!

Chapter 9

"Banks... You've got an attorney visit," Officer Mesa informed Banks as he laid in his bunk.

They still had him under investigation. It had been 21 days. From the letters Tracy sent, he knew his lawyer had been paid in full. Well, minus the trial fee, but that wasn't needed until later.

As he walked in the attorney booth, he couldn't help but smile. Joe was one clean motherfucker. Dressed in a pinstripe, charcoal Armani suit with matching Gators, Banks couldn't help but to feel inferior in his jail house oranges. *Damn, I got to get back to that bag,* he thought.

"So... What's good, B," Joe rapped.

"Man, ain't shit good but the life I'm missing," Banks replied.

"Well... Hopefully I can help you get back to it. Your girl Tracy came to pay me, but truthfully, I'd been working on your case extensively. You know, you're the only one who I'd work on their case before I get paid a dime. That's because I know you'd come through, just like you know I will. So... I found the crack!"

Banks' ears perked up. "What you got," he eagerly asked.

Joe opened his files and took a second to go over the material. He looked at Banks. "Alright... For one, the witness is full of shit, but we already knew that. She said she heard the gunshots on June 12th and saw you coming out of the house. Well, I hired an investigator, and come to find out, the victim was alive and kicking on June 14th. He was at a party in a suburban neighborhood outside of the Woodlands. Apparently, he had a white girlfriend who was in college at the time. He was spending time with her for summer break. She signed an affidavit swearing that he was at her apartment all the way until June 14th. Secondly, the gun had a partial fingerprint of yours but shit, you're a dope dealer who's touched countless amounts of firearms. That doesn't mean you've ever used one. Long story short, I got a call from the D.A. It seems Ms. Sawyer has flown the coupe."

At the mention of the State's star witness vanishing, Banks eyes' lit up. "So, what you're saying, she disappeared?"

"That's what it seems like. As of right now, no one knows where she's at," Joe confirmed.

"So, what now?"

"Well...We wait. The State will try to locate her. If they can't, their case is destroyed. They may try and push with that partial print, but they know not to meet me in the ring with that. More than likely, they'll try and plea down to about 5 to 7 years."

"Hell naw...I ain't signing for shit, Joe. I ain't do shit," Banks said vehemently.

"And you shouldn't. That's why I'ma tell them if the witness splits, you must acquit...Or in this case, dismiss."

After their talk, Banks went back to his cell. He couldn't contain his excitement. *Damn, I'm 'bout to hit the blacktop,* he told himself.

Tap-Tap. He heard the signal tap, looked on the floor and saw a kite. He opened it. It was from Serve.

"Say, young Playa. Word got back on who gave you and sis up. It was Bull. Word on the street is he got caught with a pack and folded. He didn't know exactly who was bringing shit in, so the laws tried to get you to trip yourself up. Let me know the move, Playa..."

Banks couldn't believe it was Bull. He has been feeding him since they were in the streets. Bull was one of the old crew members, and he was just like his namesake. At 5'11", 240 pounds of steel and muscle Bull was a straight up brawler. He had at least 15 KO's that Banks knew about. Even though Banks wasn't scared to knuckle up, he was relieved that the punishment for the crime had exceeded a simple beat down. Bull violated in the worst way. Snitching was a death sentence. S.O.S.—Smoke on Sight. He just had to figure out a way to get it done without getting caught. He was practically home free and the worst thing he could do was beat one murder just to catch another.

As he sat, he decided on a plan, but wasn't too sure if Tracy would go along with it. She'd been always down to play her part, but this was on another level. Bull stayed on the other side of the jail and was too game tight to fall for the sick call play. Plus, if he got caught in the holding cell when Bull got murked, ain't no way they're not hitting him with the M.

From talks with Tracy, Banks knew the captain in charge of housing and job placement had a thing for her. Captain Fuller was a potbellied white man with bald spots and a redneck. Like a lot of "good ole boys", he had a craving for dark meat. More than a few times he'd approached Tracy trying to slide between her folds. Truth be told, he was the reason the investigation on her didn't get that far. Without concrete evidence, he convinced the head Sheriff to "wait it out."

Banks now needed Tracy to "convince" Captain Fuller to move Bull to his side of the jail, and also give both of them a nighttime janitor job. That's when Banks would strike. He had 10 more days until they would have to let him off investigation. Until then, he would sit in the cell and perfect his plan to the T. When the time arrives, he'll be ready to dish out some justice.

"Sooo...You want me to fuck this white boy so he can move Bull, *and* give him a job," Tracy spat, clearly not liking the plan. Even though she wasn't too thrilled with the idea, Banks wasn't giving up.

"Look, baby...This nigga violated in a major way. How I was raised, that's unforgivable. All I'm asking of you is have your man's back. I need you, baby. He didn't just jeopardize me, but he jeopardized both of us. I told you when we first locked in, any nigga that fucks with us will get turnt to dust!"

"Brandon...2 months from now we'll be arguing and you gon' hit a bitch with that, *oh... you fucked that white boy at your job* shit. You say you not tripping now, but as soon as you get mad, I'll be all types of sluts, hoes, trash and whatever else you think about calling me," Tracy argued.

"Look, baby... On my soul, my set and my manhood, I'll never use this against you in any way. You're going against your morals and principles for me. That's loyalty at its strongest," Banks explained.

After about 10 seconds of silence, Tracy finally spoke up. "Aight, Brandon...I got you. Your ass better be lucky I love your dirty drawers."

"I love you too, Tracy." They talked some more. Banks laced her up on what needed to be done.

Tracy ended up putting that "good-good" on the captain, and within a few days, Bull was moved to the same side of the jail as Banks. On the night everything was scheduled to go down, Banks told Tracy to call in sick. That way she wouldn't be rounded up for questioning. Banks knew Bull had gym duty that night. Gym duty was always assigned to one inmate. All he had to do was sweep, then mop. For the next 3 hours after that, he'd be doing nothing but chilling and laying up.

As Bull was busy sweeping, Banks crept into the gym and used the weight set as cover. He couldn't get at him while he was sweeping because he was out in the open. Bull would see him coming. He had to be patient. He stalked his prey.

He watched Bull and a flashback of the last party they'd both been at, popped in Banks' head.

Bull had left the club that night with two bad bitches, courtesy of Banks. Now the fuck nigga decided to be a rat. The betrayal boiled over in his stomach. It felt as if steam was coming from his nostrils. As soon as Bull was done mopping, he made his way over to the area next to the weight set. There was an old mat in the utility closet the janitors used to lay down on when they were done cleaning up. This was the moment of truth.

As Bull reached for the door handle, Banks sprung from behind the weight set. He grabbed Bull by the chin, exposing his throat. With a savage swipe, he severed his aorta vein. Blood squirted. Banks continued to stab into Bulls stomach and chest repeatedly. He wanted to make sure he was sufficiently dead and send a very vivid message. *If you're a rat...You become Swiss cheese!*

Bull's body twitched and spasmed as he urinated on himself. Banks rolled him into a mat and stuffed him inside the utility closet. He then removed his outer layer of clothing. He anticipated blood being on them, so he wore 2 sets of orange jumpers. He double checked himself to make sure he was presentable.He wiped the blade clean, strapped it back to his thigh, then grabbed the broom, careful not to bump into anyone as he made his way back to his work area on B pod, where seg inmates were housed.

Once he was safely back on the tank, he gave his knife to his Latin King homeboy named KG, AKA Dragon, so he could dispose of it. "Wassup with the lawboy? Did he ask where I was at," Banks inquired.

KG looked up at the picket. "Hell naw. That fool was sleep the whole time," KG replied.

Good. He'll have to say I was on the tank all night. If he says he doesn't know, he'll have to explain why. And he's not about to tell them he was sleeping, Banks thought.

2 hours later, an alarm sounded and the jail was being put on administrative lock down.

"What's going on," Banks asked innocently as they retrieved all the workers and escorted them back to their blocks.

Captain Fuller looked at him accusingly and said, "It seems an inmate has been stabbed to death in the gym. Right now, the whole jail is on lockdown until an investigation can be conducted."

As he walked back to his cell, he couldn't help but wonder if he covered all his tracks. Did he forget something? Did anyone happen to see? Only time would tell. If he *did* make a mistake, there was nothing he could do about it now. He figured he might as well get some sleep. That night, he slept like a newborn baby. He dreamt about slamming Cadillac doors and Macking top-shelf whores!

***

"Oohh fuuucckk! Shit! Damn, nigga, you're beating this pussy up!" Even though she was playing a very dangerous game, Dorian couldn't deny the fact that Dread had some serious dick game. He texted her earlier, knowing she was at Paccy's crib and told her to meet him at the corner store. She quickly thought of an excuse to leave. Going so far as to ask Paccy if he needed her to grab anything from the store.

"Naw, I'm good," he said as she rushed out the door.

That was 13 minutes ago. Now, she was bent over, on the side of the gas station. Skirt flipped over her ass with her panties down to her ankles. The only thing blocking the view were their parked cars. Dread opened her ass cheeks apart and continued to dig off into her snatch. "Shit, Dread! You're fucking my pussy up!" Dorian could never get used to the savage dick Dread slung around.

He grabbed her by the ponytail. "Bitch! Who do you belong to?"

"You, Dread...I belong to you," she declared as her ass clapped against his stomach.

Looking down at her booty jiggle, Dread allowed a dribble of spit to fall and land in the crack of her ass. He massaged it around the rim of her asshole before inserting a thumb into her backdoor. He knew that always sets her off.

"Oohh fuuckk! I'm 'bout to cream all on that dick...Ooh shit...I'm cummminnngggg!" True to her words, Dorian rained nut all over Dread's thighs and balls. Wave after wave raked through her whole body. She reached back up under them, grabbed hold of his nuts and messaged them.

"Agh... Agh... Shit! Bitch, I'm 'bout to cum," Dread growled. "Open up!"

Dorian hopped off the dick, turned around, grabbed his slimy stick and engulfed it. She feverishly stroked him until he tilted back and unloaded jets of white, hot cum down her throat.

As soon as Dread was emptied, he pushed her head out the way. "Bitch, you're dismissed!" That was the third time they had done something since Dread had sent her the recording. To be honest, she enjoyed it while it was going on, but afterwards, she always felt like shit. Each time, she hated Dread a little more for making her do it. She was beginning to fall in love with Paccy, and Dread had her feeling like a slimy ass bitch.

She hopped inside her new Lexus LS 430 Paccy bought her and silently cried. *Shit,* she thought. *I almost forgot the blunt wraps...And some baby wipes for my coochie.* Afterwards, she visited the fish spot and grabbed her and Paccy some catfish and fries as well as a shrimp basket.

Even though he claimed he didn't want anything to eat, Dorian couldn't see herself returning home with nothing for him. As she headed home, it hit her. She knew exactly how she would deal with the Dread problem. It was going to take a little conniving on her part, but shit, that was her specialty.

She quickly picked up her phone, scrolled down until she saw Chrissy's number.

After 3 rings, Chrissy answered. "Heyyy, bitch!"

"Wassup, hoe! What you been up to?" Dorian needed to small talk before she got to the meat of the matter.

"Shit... I've been working like crazy to stack that bread up," Chrissy told her.

Dorian let her ramble on about her job for a little while before she hit her with the punchline. "So, check game, C. Do you wanna make some money," Dorian asked.

"What? What kind of question is that? That's like asking a fish would you like a drink of water? What do you got in mind?"

"Do you still have NOB's number?" Dorian crossed her fingers, hoping that she did indeed have it.

"Yeah, I still got it. Why? Wassup?"

NOB was a young Blood nigga from New Orleans that had migrated to Houston before Katrina hit. 6'5", rail thin, dark, dreaded up with a fetish for gun smoke. He openly admitted that he was no drug dealer. His way to wealth was robbery and homicide. *That's* how he made his living.

A while ago, he'd approached Dorian and Chrissy while they were shopping at the Galleria. It was right before her world had turned tragically upside down. She admitted that he was cute, and she was feeling his gangsta, but it didn't seem as if he was getting any real money. She stored him under *Reserves*. Dorian went on to explain her plan, and after a short pause, Chrissy expressed her concerns.

"Bitch, you know if anything goes wrong, we're dead," Chrissy pointed out.

"Yeah, but I got the nigga eating out the crotch of my panties," Dorian arrogantly expressed. "So, he won't suspect a thing. I just need NOB to handle his end."

"Aight, D, I'll hit him up. What's the breakdown? You know he gon' want to know that before he agrees to anything."

"60 percent for him. You and I will spit 40 since he's going to be doing all the heavy lifting."

"I think he'll go for that," Chrissy admitted.

"Bet!" And with that, Dorian hung up the phone. Now that she put the play in motion, she needed to lay down the groundwork.

As she entered the condo she and Paccy shared, she tiptoed through the kitchen to eavesdrop on his conversation. From what it sounded like, he was discussing business. She placed her plate in the microwave, then went to take her bath. Hopefully, she could tighten up her coochie just in case Paccy wanted to get him some. After a vinegar-soaked bath, she walked into the bedroom and noticed Paccy counting large stacks of money. She also noticed his FN *and* his AK were in arms reach.

He looked up and smiled. "Wassup, boo?"

Lately, his smile alone would make her heart sputter. She knew she was in love, but she wouldn't dare tell him for fear that the love wouldn't be reciprocated. "Nothing, babe. Are you headed out?"

"Yeah... I gotta go handle some bidness real quick. I won't be gone long though."

Dorian picked up a hot pink fingernail polish and began to paint her nails. She usually went to the nail shop, but while she was in the tub, she purposely broke each one. So now, she sported the natural look. She seductively walked up to Paccy and positioned herself directly in front of him. He stopped what he was doing. His eyes traveled from her toned legs up to her camel toe. After lingering there for a few seconds, his eyes traveled further up north until he was left staring into her eyes.

Dorian smiled, licked her lips and said, "Would you like for me to suck your dick before you go? I would hate for you to be out there with a sack full of nut."

Paccy couldn't get enough of Dorian. He loved a freak, and when it came to freaks, she was Queen Bee. After arranging another stack into the duffle bag, he leaned back and allowed Dorian to do what she did best.

Just as she grabbed a hold of him, she accidentally bumped the fingernail polish over, and the polish dripped onto the cash he still had left out the bag. "Oops... My bad, babe. I'm sooo sorry," she pleaded.

"It's all good. It ain't shit but nail polish. This shit gon' spend the same way," Paccy assured her. "Now...What were you saying? You don't want me to be out there with what?"

With a smirk, Dorian dropped to her knees and devoured every inch of his manhood. After he came down her throat, he grabbed his stuff, made a few quick calls and was out the door.

5 minutes after he left, Dorian received a text message.

Chrissy: Just tlkd 2 NOB. He's down but wants 2 tlk 2 u 1st.

Dorian : Bet..Tell him hit me up.

Minutes later, NOB called and Dorian gave him the necessary info. He explained to her how it would all go down. Either it was his way or no way. After all, he was the one in the line of fire. She reluctantly agreed. She had an uneasiness about the whole ordeal, but Dread had backed her into a corner. It was too late to turn back now. Once she hung up, she laid in bed and thought about what Chrissy had said. *"If this don't work, we're dead!"*

"This has to work," she whispered to herself as she drifted off into a troubled sleep.

Chapter 10

Club Heat was off the chain once again. Paccy and the IGF were in full effect. It seemed like everyone in attendance had a bottle of Rosé or Ace of Spades. Each member of his crew had at least one female on their arm who was guaranteed to give up the goods at the end of the night.

Dressed in a midnight blue Hermes body suit with all-white St. Laurent pumps, white and gold LV clutch, VS diamonds sparkling off her wrist and ears, Dorian watched as her boo Paccy commanded the crowd.

Decked in blue and white Robin jeans, white patent leather Ferragomo sneakers, white and blue checkered Ferragamo belt, no shirt, showing off countless tattoos, his VS1's blinding the club, Paccy stood like the great general Hannibal after a victorious battle.

Right below him were 3 groupies waiting for a chance to catch the sauce that dripped off of him. Dorian couldn't help but to smirk.

Before they left the house, she made sure every ounce of cum was drained from his sack. Her phone vibrated. She had a text message.

Blocked: Mens restroom 10 min.

"Fuck!" She cursed herself. Dread was on some straight fuck shit. *Don't he know, this is the same as rape,* she wondered as she made her way back to the bar. As she approached, she noticed Chrissy and some fine ass white girl working their ass off, trying to accommodate everyone's drink orders.

When Chrissy saw her walking up, she gave Dorian an inquisitive look. *This wasn't part of the plan!* As if reading her thoughts, Dorian looked at her and said, "Bitch, change of plans! This nigga's on some fuck shit. He wants me to fall off in the men's restroom."

"What? While Paccy and the whole IGF is here? I know you not 'bout to do that, D. That's suicide!" Chrissy wisely advised her.

"Man, I know. That's why he wants to do it in the restroom. He knows someone will walk in. There's no way I could have a good excuse for being in the men's restroom, other than I was tryna get fucked!"

"So, what's the play now?" Chrissy asked.

"Look, go ahead and give me the drink."

Chrissy handed her a bottle of champagne.

"I'll hit you on the hip and let you know the next move." With that, Dorian took off and headed in the direction of the *women's'* restroom. Minutes later, a text flashed across her screen.

Blocked: Where u at bitch? Don't play with me.

Dorian: I'm n da women's' restroom. If u want it, cum get it. U know I ain't 'bout to rock out in no men's restroom, Dread!

Blocked: I don't give a fuck where u wanna rock out at. If u don't make it over here in 10 seconds. Bro will c all footage

Damn, she thought. She was hoping she wouldn't have to, but...She took a deep breath and made her way to the men's restroom. Luckily for her, it was almost empty. It was one heavy set dude at the urinal, and another light skinned dude at the sink washing his hands. Neither one noticed her. No doubt, they assumed she was just another man entering the stalls.

Dread stood in one of the stalls. The door opened, with a mug on his face. She hurried in with him.

"You're wrong for this Dread," she whispered.

"Naw bitch, you wrong...For fucking my nigga behind my back. Now, do what you do best," he commanded as he pushed her down onto the toilet.

She looked up at him. "Well, at least hold my drink. And don't drink my shit...I just bought it," she told him as she handed over the bottle. With a smirk on his face, Dread took a large swig of the expensive champagne. After seeing him drink from her bottle, Dorian put her head down, smirked, then went to work on his knob.

Sucking. Slurping. With one hand on his balls, massaging and kneading them. Spit and pre cum leaked out the corners of her mouth as she tried desperately to make his King Cobra spit up venom.

Dread began to grit his teeth. He grabbed the back of her head, face fucking her with every inch of steel he could fit. She took it all like a champ, expanding her throat. Allowing him to have his way.

The door to the stall attempted to swing open, but Dread was in the way. "My bad, homie. I ain't know somebody was in here," a familiar voice explained.

Oh shit! That's Paccy, Dorian realized.

Sensing her anxiety, Dread called out," It's just me in here with this skeezer ass thot. She sucks dick like a porn star though...You wanna try her out?" With a mouth full of cock and pleading eyes, Dorian shook her head, praying that Dread would chill out.

"Naw, cuz. You know wifey would kill me if she found out I stepped out on her. Especially at the same party she was at," Paccy admitted.

"Suit yourself, cuz. Matter fact, where's wifey at? She needs to put a nigga in the door with her homegirl," Dread called out as he continued to pump in and out of Dorians' mouth. She closed her eyes and allowed him to abuse her throat, in hopes Paccy would be gone by the time Dread was finished.

"Shit, I don't know. Probably on the dance floor, but I'm 'bout to go find her though." With that, Paccy left the bathroom.

Mere seconds later, Dread gripped her head tightly, tilted his head back and unloaded a huge glob of nut into her mouth. She struggled to swallow it all down.

"Agghhh Fuuuckk," Dread announced as his balls emptied. "Whooo. Damn girl, your head game is off da fucking chain! I'm never gone be able to let that go," Dread commented as he zipped up his Tru Religion jeans. He looked at the top of Dorian's head and dropped the near empty bottle into her lap.

"When he finds out though, you're as good as dead. I just hope I'm the one that pulls the trigger." With that, he left her sitting on the toilet. What he didn't see was the tears that streamed from her eyes.

She felt hurt. While Paccy was turning down pussy because of the love and respect he had for her, she was letting his patna buss all down her throat. *Maybe I deserve to die,* she thought as she got up, grabbed the tissue and cleaned the corners of her mouth. She took out two mint Altoids and popped them.

After composing herself, she snuck out of the restroom. As she was leaving, she accidentally bumped into one of the groupies that were worshipping Paccy earlier that night. She smiled at the thought of the groupie getting curved.

"Bitch," she heard her say, as the woman rushed into the bathroom. Dorian made it over to the bar and gave Chrissy the signal to proceed to stage 2 of the plan.

As the club was closing, each crew member stumbled out of Club Heat with their arm draped over their choice of the night. In some cases, two women decorated the inside of their whip. Dread was always one that could handle his liquor, but for some reason tonight, he was losing that battle. As he miraculously reached his metallic blue Range Rover, Chrissy seemingly materialized out of thin air.

"Heyyy sexy," she purred. Dread recognized her as the fine ass bartender he was unsuccessfully trying to mack on earlier. He tried his best to shake back and regain his composure.

"Wh..Wassup. Wi..Wit it," he slurred. "Wh..What you got pl...Planned for tonight?"

Chrissy leaned in and whispered, "I want to go home with you, but I don't know. You seem too drunk to drive, much less fuck!" Hearing the prospect of getting some brand-new pussy, Dread straightened up and tried his best to appear sober.

"If you feel I'm too drunk to drive." Dread took the keys and handed them to her. "Then you drive!" If he wasn't so fucked up, Dread wouldn't have allowed anyone, especially someone he just met to drive his shit. The last thing he remembered was hoping inside his truck. Once the A/C hit him, he was out like a light.

BOOM! As Dorian rode Paccy into sexual bliss, the door to their condo was kicked in. Three masked shooters invaded their home. Before Paccy could reach for his strap, the lead shooter ran up and smacked him with the barrel of the .45!

WHAP!

"Agghhh shit!" Paccy cried out. Blood leaking from an open gash on the side of his head. Dorian attempted to scream, but was backhanded, falling to the floor, writhing in pain.

With the pistol aimed at Paccys' head, the lead gunman asked, "Where's the money and work at, bitch nigga?"

Paccy debated on playing hardball. They had masks on. Being a jack boy himself, he knew they had intended on it being *just* a simple robbery. He looked towards Dorian and saw fear in her eyes. If he was completely honest with himself, then he'd have to admit he was in love with her. Because of that, he couldn't stomach the thought of him being the reason something bad happened to her.

"Say fam, I don't keep work in here, but I got a lil' bread in the bedroom," Paccy informed them.

The gunman forced Paccy onto his feet and told his companion, "Watch the bitch". The two of them made their way to the back bedroom. As he was being shoved, Paccy couldn't help but wonder. One, who had the balls to try and rob him? Two, how the fuck did he get caught slipping?

As he reached the safe, the gunman smacked him in the back of the head for good measure.

"Aghhh...What the fuck nigga?" Paccy screamed in pain and frustration.

"Open it up!" The gunman ordered, pistol leveled at the back of his skull. Paccy knelt before the safe, blood gushing from the gashes in his head. He swore to himself he would murder *everyone* that was involved. The blood continued to pour down his scalp, into his eyes, binding him.

As he turned the combination, he heard Dorian scream from the living room. He closed his eyes and made a quick prayer. *Just make it out alive,* he told himself.

The door to the safe swung open. "Here...Take this and fill it up," the gunman told Paccy, tossing him an empty pillowcase. "Oh and go ahead and put all that ice you and your bitch got in the bag. Also, Say D2 I need you in here. Bring the bitch with you!" D2 appeared with Dorian in tow.

Together, they zip tied the couple. Paccy and Dorian watched helplessly as the gunman relieved them of all their money and jewelry. The whole time, Paccy just sat there fuming while murder and malice infected his soul.

The whole ordeal took no more than thirty minutes tops. What was odd to Paccy, the jackers left both of them their cell phones. That was definitely not in the jack boy manual. He couldn't believe it. Someone tried him! Not only that, but they tried him in front of his bitch. He was furious, not to mention extremely embarrassed. He wouldn't stop until whoever responsible *and* all they're family members were dead.

After three hours of blowing up his cell phone and not getting any answers, one of Paccys' top soldiers named J Bang, decided to stop by to check on his big homie. As he pulled up, he noticed the front door to the spot was kicked wide open. With his gun drawn, he cautiously entered.

He searched the front room, then ventured to the back bedroom. That's where he found them, zip tied and helpless. After he cut them loose, Paccy ordered him to keep his mouth shut. "Don't tell nobody shit 'bout this," he said.

Paccy grabbed his phone and called his top lieutenant. The phone rang, then went to voicemail. He tried again. This time it went straight to voicemail, as if someone forwarded the call. *What the fuck?,* he thought. He didn't want to believe it, but it seemed like Dread was avoiding his calls. He had an eerie feeling in his gut. His street senses were telling him something was up. He just didn't know what.

He decided to call his other capos and ordered an emergency meeting. He didn't want to say too much over the phone, so he just told them to meet up at "The Zoo".

Summit Point aka "The Zoo" was the headquarters for the IGF. No other gang in the city would be caught near The Zoo. Not without consequences. He tried to call Dread once again, with the same result. He shook it off and got ready to hold the meeting.

Meanwhile, after picking up Dread's phone and sending Paccy to voicemail, Chrissy picked up her phone and dialed NOB. "Where you wanna meet at," he asked.

"Meet me on I-10 and Uvalde right there at the Subway," she answered. She was pretty confident Dread would be knocked out for the next five hours. Courtesy of a cocktail of Xan bars and oxytocin pills crushed and poured into a bottle of expensive champagne. The same bottle that Dorian took to the restroom.

As Chrissy pulled up to the subway, she noticed NOB's charger double parked. She maneuvered her Beamer, parked next to him then jumped in his backseat. "So, I see everything went how it was supposed to," she commented.

"Yeah, it was a breeze. I got y'all's cut right here." NOB motioned for the passenger to hand him the duffle bag. "That's forty bands for y'all. It was a dollar flat. I kept his jewelry though. Since that wasn't part of the deal," NOB said, while checking his surroundings.

"You good on *his* jewelry. We just wanted the cash. Did you notice what we told you to look for?"

"Oh yeah, I did. It's all in there," NOB assured her.

As she was exiting the car, NOB spoke up. "Say Chrissy, when you gone let a real nigga see what that's pussy bout!"

Chrissy looked back and smirked. "You got to pay to play, lil' whodie!"

NOB laughed. "I work *too* hard for mine, to trick it off."

"Well baby boy, I guess there goes your answer," Chrissy responds as she closes his back door, then hops in her whip. She looked in the bag to make sure she had the right money. After she confirmed it was, she picked up the phone and texted Dorian.

Chrissy: Hey Bitch. Hit me when u get up.

That was code to let Dorian know she had the bread. Now, it was time to move to phase three.

Chapter 11

It had been three weeks since Bull got murdered. The whole jail had been on a 3-day lockdown, while homicide detectives tried to figure things out. They spent entire days pulling people out of their cells to question them. Banks wasn't worried about witnesses. The only people that knew were Tracy, Serve and his Latin King homie. It was almost shift change. He knew his baby was about to be coming in. He got up and got himself ready.

After brushing his teeth, washing his face and getting his waves in order, Banks turned on the radio and listened to the news.

"Today, D.E.A. agents apprehended who they believed to be the main supplier for a Houston based cartel called The MOB de Muerte. Raul Henejosa was indicted on 322 counts of conspiracy, distribution, extortion among other things. He's also believed to be personally responsible for 6 murders as well as overseeing many more. US attorney Jonh Carry told reporters, the US government will not stand for domestic terrorism, and will be pursuing the death penalty."

"What the fuck?" Banks mumbled to himself. He couldn't believe what he was hearing. His plug Raul was up shit creek without a paddle. He couldn't help but to think, maybe he was lucky for coming to jail when he did. No doubt, he would have been wrapped up in all that bullshit too.

With his plug gone for what may be forever, he had no intentions of finding a new one. It seemed like the game had made its final move to show him where he belonged. Luckily for him, Joe was paid. Now he had to figure out how he was going to get his bag back right.

As he sat back, he mapped it out in his head. Someone yelled "shift change" over the run. He stood up and looked through the small window of his cell door. Sure enough, standing like a thoroughbred, uniform pants so tight, you could see her pussy lips poking through the fabric. Hair done, nails done, everything did.

His dick began to twitch. When she looked towards his cell and smiled, he couldn't help it. He reached into his boxers and gave his dick a nice squeeze. *Damn, I need some pussy!*

They'd been fucking around for a little over a year and a half, and they still haven't had sex. Not to any fault of their own. The way the tank is set up, it's damn near impossible for them to fuck around and no inmate not be able to see them. They couldn't risk the potential of someone taking them down like that.

The only thing they had to relieve the tension, was long passionate nights of phone sex, but even that was getting played out. Banks had repeatedly told Tracy that she had every right to go out there and get some dick since he was locked up, but she continued to claim she would wait for him. Now that the business was concluded, Banks needed some wet pussy or mouth to penetrate. If tricking was his thing, he would have been paid for it. But it wasn't!

That's it! He figured out how to get the trial money for Joe, plus some money for when he touched down. He didn't want to come out on his ass. He wasn't sure how Tracy was going to take it. *Could I really stomach it,* he asked himself. Him and Tracy had come a long way, and he could honestly say that he loved her. Could he do what he contemplated on doing?

As he watched her move around the picket, occasionally popping her booty and licking her lips for him, he decided.

Hell yeah he could stomach it. After all, if she was ride or die like he felt she was, she would be down with it anyway.

Later that night, after he felt she had made it home safely. He hit her cellphone.

"Heyy Daddy," she answered with excitement.

"Wassup baby?...You at the crib already?"

"Yeah, I just got out the shower...Damn your deep ass voice always gets my pussy creaming," she admitted.

"Oh yeah. I can't lie, today you had my dick hard as hell with that show you was putting on in the picket."

"Is that right," she purred. Banks didn't want the conversation to get off track.

"Look baby, I need to talk to you 'bout something."

"What's up baby? What's wrong," she immediately became concerned.

"You know Joe came to see me. He feels like he'll bring me home, but I told him I'm not signing for shit. Now, we already took care of the initial fee, but if we have to go to trial, I want that bread already put to the side."

"Yeah, I know boo. I tried to get more with the loan, but they were talking 'bout since I still owed on the cosign for my lil' brother car, they didn't want to give me more than what they did. But we can keep doing what we been doing baby," she suggested.

"Well, not really. I haven't told you yet, but the feds ran down on Raul. They hit him with all types of charges. I guess it's safe to say that's over with."

"Damn...For real?" She was shocked to hear the news. During her trips to go pick up for Banks, she had become fond of Raul. He treated her like family. "So, what do we do now? I need you home ASAP baby!"

"Look... I hope you don't take this the wrong way. I want you to start stripping." He didn't want to sugarcoat shit, so he just came right out and said what was on his mind.

Tracy slunk back in surprise. "You want me too what, nigga!"

"Baby...Before you say no. Just give me a chance to explain why I feel like that's our route.

"I'm listening, nigga. This shit better be good!"

"You got bitches out there making fifteen hundred to two grand a night. You the baddest bitch in the city, so I know you won't have no trouble making that," he tried to finesse.

"Whatever, nigga. Don't try to flatter me. It ain't gone work, so just stick to the facts," she countered.

"Naw, for real boo. We've come too far to fall short now. Daddy needs you," he spat.

"So, what about this job? You want me to quit?"

"No," he replied quickly. "You can hit the club when you leave here on the weekend and on your days off." Silence enveloped the phone.

"I don't know 'bout that Brandon...I mean, Damn! You ain't asking a bitch to work extra hours at a burger joint. You want a bitch to buss it open in front of a bunch of random ass niggas!"

Sensing he was close to convincing her, he went in for the kill. " Boo...It ain't gone be for too long. If you make $500 a night, then that's $15,000 for a month. Making that type of bread, we'll have everything we need to make sure I'm home free. I know you want a nigga home."

"Don't play me, Brandon. You know I want you home. What kind of shit is that? I've been risking my life and freedom to bring you home. Sshhhit! Man look. I don't want to hear any jealousy shit. You want me to bring you home...By any means? Are you *really* good with that?"

"What?...Hell yeah, I'm aight with that. I *need* to be home with you baby," he countered.

"Psshh...Aight. I'll go to Bottoms Up and see what's up after we get off the phone."

"That's my girl," he said excitedly.

"Nigga stop smiling," she said teasingly. That made Banks smile even more. They talked about what she could expect working at the club. Even though Banks had never pimped, or mack'd for that matter, he had soaked up a lot of game from Serve. He felt confident he could lead her in the right direction. Before they hung up, he wished her luck as she got herself ready to go tackle the game.

What Banks didn't know, Tracy had a taste of the stripper pole. When she was 15, she ran away from home. Her uncle kept trying to feel up on her newly developed body. Even though she wasn't old enough to drive, she drove grown men wild. Of course, she would never let them know her true age. With the help of her friend's older sister's ID, she was able to convince them that she was 18. As she jumped in the shower, she reminisced about how she got introduced to the game a long time ago.

The music was blasting. Thick gray clouds of smoke polluted the air. If you didn't do drugs, you were still liable to get high off the contact. Tracy's friends' older sister Monica was throwing what she called a trick or treat party. At the time, Tracy didn't understand why she would call it that. She didn't see any bowls of candy or any costumes of any kind.

It wasn't too packed, but there were quite a few people in that small 3-bedroom apartment. Tracy started to sweat as she backed her plump booty onto a helpless young cat, who had his back against the wall. Kanye Wests' "Mercy" blared over the stereo. Tracy worked her ass in a circle, while looking back at him and licking her lips. She could feel his dick rock up, and her panties became moist.

Even though she was young, she had already been fucking and sucking. The cat she held hostage was 20 years old, tall, brown skin with a few tattoos on his neck and arms. He wore his hair in a taper fade with a design going down one side. Of course, he didn't know she was so young. The party was supposed to be all strippers. She definitely wasn't going to tell him.

Monica knew her sister Courtney and her friend Tracy were too young to be at this type of party, but she was too busy worrying about one thing. *Money!*

Monica Scott aka Money was what most niggas called a money hungry bitch. She believed the only thing a man could do for her was one, give her money and two, make her cum. In that order and that order only.

Twice a month, she would call her stripper friends and throw what she called "Trick or Treat" parties. If you were in attendance, then it was understood that you were there to trick your money off. In return, you got your nut off any way you wanted. Head, pussy, ass...*Whatever* your pleasure.

So while Tracy was working her underage ass in the living room, Monica was in the bedroom getting triple teamed. While a pair of brothers sawed into her pussy and ass, their first cousin rammed his dick down Money's throat. If they thought she would back down or tap out, they were in for a rude awakening.

She slurped, sucked and licked until the cousin roared back and unloaded all over her face. Without missing a beat, she grabbed a towel she had just for that purpose, wiped her face and continued to ride the brothers until their nuts swelled, and they filled their magnum condoms.

Not to be outdone, one of Monica's road dawgs named Alexis had just made $5,000 for an hour's worth of work. Not bad! They still had all night, and many others were waiting on their turn with the 15 lovely ladies of the evening.

"What's your name," old boy whispered in Tracy's ear. His dick was hard as steel. She felt it poking at her lower back.

"Tracy," she replied shyly.

"Well...How 'bout we dip off real quick so we can blow some Loud? It's too crowded in here for me."

After she thought about it, she decided to say fuck it. She wanted to find Courtney first so she could tell her she was leaving. She entered Courtney's room and what she saw, shocked her to her core. Sitting on the bed was her 10th grade math teacher, Mr. Allen. Between his legs, was her best friend Courtney with her head in his lap. "Oh shit. My bad," Tracy stammered.

"I thought you locked the door," Mr. Allen scolded Courtney. She picked her head and saw Tracy's look of shock.

"Heyy girl," Courtney shyly acknowledged. Pre cum and spit covered her mouth and chin.

Tracy, feeling embarrassed, rushed out the room and straight through the front door. Not before grabbing her dance partner. After blowing a Loud stick, their conversation led to sex. Not soon after, Tracy was getting her young pussy beaten to a pulp behind an abandoned house. In her short life span, she had sex with 5 different dudes. None of them compared to the dicking down she received that night.

She came twice and assumed when they were done, he would leave without a word. Instead, he gave her $300. *Wow,* she thought. Good dick and she got paid? Since that day, she'd been hooked. She later convinced Money to get her on at the club, in exchange for Tracy giving her 20 percent of what she made every night for a week straight. So at 15 years old, Tracy made a living shaking her ass.

She thought she was through with all that. Now her man needed her. She just couldn't let him find out, she'd *been* shaking ass and selling pussy. As she pulled up in the parking lot of her former kingdom, her pussy began to tingle. Just the thought of all the money to be made, had her creaming in herself.

Money made her cum. She hadn't met a man yet, that had a pole attached to his body, that would make her cum more or harder than that pole attached to the stage. Maybe Banks will be the first.

As she hopped out her new cherry red Nissan Altima, the bouncer instantly smiled. Even though the parking lot was packed, he still recognized Tracy Jones aka Sparkle. He better. He'd been trying to get up in her drawers since she started working there 5-6 years ago. The closest he'd gotten, was licking her fingers after she had played with her pussy on stage. He subconsciously licked his lips as if he could still taste her on his tongue.

"Hey Greg," she greeted as she neared the entrance of the club.

"What's up Spark. I see you decided to come back home. Everybody said you wouldn't come back after the incident.

The incident he was referring to was when Tracy stomped a mud hole in another stripper for going in her purse. The other chick, whose name was Cream, was up under some pimping. She had a horrible night, but instead of facing her pimp broke, she decided to take matters into her own hands...Literally! *Big Mistake!*

Tracy walked in and caught her with her hand in the cookie jar. When she was done with her, Cream had a broken jaw, a cracked rib, and a puncture wound from the heel of Tracy's 4-inch stilettos. She told herself then, it was time to leave the game. She became a jailer, but now she was back.

"Yeah G, I'm back. Hopefully not for too long though. Where's Ant at?"

"He's in the office and I hope not for long turns into no time soon."

Tracy took a deep breath before heading inside to see the manager. A man she happened to be former fuck buddies with. Anthony aka Ant Dawg. He wasn't too pleased about her leaving last time and they hadn't really spoken since then. She wasn't sure how he would feel about her coming back. Tracy knocks on the office door.

***

You can feel the tension in that small, cramped apartment as 7 members of one of the most ruthless crews in the city assemble. Each member listened attentively, as their leader demanded some answers. Paccy passed up each one, making sure to look them in the eyes, determined to pick up any sign of guilt. All of his trusted officers were present except one.

Dread had been by his side since day one. He never missed a meeting. Just as his thoughts lingered off, Paccy's phone rang. "Many Men" by 50 Cent announced the caller, knowing exactly who's calling, he answered the phone. Going in!

"Nigga, where the fuck you at? I've been blowing up your shit all fucking day!"

"Damn...My bad Cuz, I passed out. I just got up right now and seen you had hit me," Dread explained groggily. "Where you at?"

"We all at the Zoo, waiting on you!" Paccy growled into the phone.

"Aight. Well, I'm on the way Cuz. Let me grab something to eat. Man, I passed out in my whip. I woke up on some back street in front of a Vaco. I'm on the way now though."

Paccy figured he would wait until Dread arrived to tell him about the jack move. 20 minutes later, Dread pulled up. Paccy noticed he still had on the same clothes from the night before. He knew Dread never wore the same clothes 2 days in a row. Paccy felt a little more at ease, but still wasn't all the way convinced.

After they embraced, Dread took notice of the scene before him. The tension was thick as Johnni Blaze. "What's crackin...You sounded a lil' stressed out on the phone."

Paccy took a second before he replied. Making sure to look Dread dead in the eyes. "I got robbed last night, homie. Niggas kicked in my shit and got me for a hundred bands plus me and my girl's jewelry. What I'm tripping on... Only the niggas in this room knew where I laid my head at. So, I'm looking for answers."

Dread picked up on the insinuation. He looked Paccy in the eyes and said, "Straight up Cuz, you know ain't shit like that going on this way. I ain't neva been on no fuck shit with you. You have my word that if anyone of the homies had anything to do with it, I'm a body their ass myself!"

Paccy felt in his heart Dread was telling the truth, so he turned his attention to the others. Just then, his phone vibrates. He received a text message.

Unknown: Dread got you for your paper. Check in his trunk, under his clothes.

What the fuck, Paccy thought. His heart began to pound in his chest. *It can't be. This got to be some type of mistake,* he kept repeating in his head, over and over. He stared at Dread as he was talking to another one of the crew members named Bam. His nostrils flared open. His breathing became heavy.

"Yo Dread...Let me borrow your truck real quick. I need to make a run and I don't have no gas in my shit. Not thinking twice about it, Dread tossed him the keys to the Range. Paccy immediately went outside and inspected the truck. He was desperately hoping his long-time friend didn't cut his throat like that. He searched the back, underneath the dirty clothes and his fears were realized.

His heart dropped as he discovered 3 stacks of bills hidden. He knew immediately it was his money, because of the fingernail polish Dorian accidentally spilled on it the night before. "Bitch ass shit!" He growled. He had no choice. He couldn't believe Dread bit the hand that fed him.

He picked up the phone and dialed Bam's number. "Ayyee," Bam answered.

"Bam, where's Dread at," Paccy asked.

"Shit...He's right here, Cuz."

"I need you and him to come out here real quick. Don't tell the others, but I found out who got me for my bread. I need y'all two to ride." Paccy tried his best to hide his emotions.

"Bet...We on the way!"

Moments later, Dread and Bam emerged from the apartment. "So, who we gotta spank," Dread asked while rubbing his hands together. Paccy looked at Dread. With a sneer, he threw the stacks of money at him. Confused, Dread looked at the money, then looked at Paccy.

"Cuz...I don't understand... What the fuck is this," he asked bewildered.

"Come on D...That's how you do me," Paccy spat. Upon hearing the revelation, Bam upped his .40 Beretta and had it leveled with Dread's head.

"Hold up," Dread pleaded. "I don't know what you talking 'bout Cuz. I'd never steal from you!"

"Oh yeah? Well why was it in your trunk then nigga?"

Dread froze. "My trunk," he whispered to himself in disbelief. His mind began to race. Finally, it hit him. Before he could tell Paccy who'd set him up, Paccy pulled his .50 Desert Eagle and *BOCKA*, blew half of Dread's head off his shoulders.

Pieces of his cranium littered the pavement. A couple of his dreadlocks laid bloody underneath an old Ford Escort. If you didn't know any better, you'd think someone dropped noodles and tomato sauce all over the parking lot.

"Y'all clean that nigga up," Paccy ordered Bam as he solemnly walked back into the condo. He'd just lost his best friend. He knew he'd never be the same again. An hour later, Dread's body was being burned to a crisp, along with his metallic blue Range.

Paccy really didn't have any cash left, but he had plenty of work. After getting off the bricks he had, as well as collecting all past due balances, he was roughly at $400,000. The only problem was his connect Raul had just went to the feds, so he needed a new plug.

"I'm telling you Cuz, that nigga's legit," Bam told him as they sat in the spot. Bam claimed he came across a new plug through his cousin Meesha. He claimed her baby daddy was a Haitian cat named Pierre. Everyone knew Pierre was pushing weight, but he hadn't wanted to fuck with Paccy because they had a bad reputation for robbing their plugs.

Bam claimed it was his cousin's baby daddy, but really it was his jump off Toya's cousin. Some nigga named Ron. He knew Paccy would have never gone for it if he would have told him the truth, so he lied. He'd been messing with Toya for 6 months, so he felt he could trust her. "Say Bam, I can't afford to take no L's lil' homie. Especially after what Dreads punk ass did," Paccy warned. Clearly receiving the intended threat, Bam assured him that they wouldn't.

"Cuz...I got you. Pierre's like family. I told him we needed a plug. He said he got me, but he only wants to deal with me." Paccy already figured that. He knew his reputation, so he wasn't surprised when certain players didn't want to deal with him directly. They say you're not supposed to shit where you eat, unless you're content with eating shit.

Paccy agreed and told Bam to set the buy up for 16 birds at 24k a piece. That would be pretty much everything he had. If anything went wrong, he would be flat broke. But Bam would be dead! He handed the money over to Bam and told him "Get at me ASAP!"

As he pulled off, Bam called Toya. No answer. "What the fuck! Bitch answer the phone!" He tried again. After 4 rings, Toya finally answered, sounding as if she just got through running a marathon.

"Ughh..He..Hello?"

"Mannn. What the fuck took you so long to answer the phone," Bam grilled.

"My bad babe. I was on the treadmill working out. You know I got to keep this body and pussy right and tight for you," Toya sang. Bam's dick began to rise as he thought about Toya in some tights, sweating, pussy bussing out the fabric. Her 40-inch ass and 36 B cup titties bouncing to and fro!

Ever since they met, he couldn't keep his hands off her. She was a certified freak. Just the way he liked them. He began to tell himself that she just may be the one.

"Well look...Go ahead and call your cousin and tell him that it's a go for the 16. I'm in traffic right now," Bam instructed. When he didn't get an immediate response, he looked at the phone to make sure the call didn't drop. *Nope, still connected.* "Hello?...Hello?..Toya, you still there?"

"Yeah, yeah...I'm still her babe."

"Did you hear what I said," he asked suspiciously.

"Yeah..You said to call my cousin and let him know it's a go for the 16 and that you're in traffic right now. What time you coming by cause you know I need some of daddy's dick!," she asked seductively.

Bam looked at his Johnny the Jeweler watch. "Give me about an hour," he said before he hung up.

From experience, she knew an hour meant two and a half. Yet and still, she planned on having the big dick nigga out her crib in 45 minutes. As she hung up the phone, she looked her baby daddy NOB in the eyes and said, "Did you hear that? He said he wants me to tell *you* he needs 16 of them thangs." Then she dove back into his lap, to finish what she was doing before she was rudely interrupted.

NOB sat back with one hand on Toya's head, pushing her down, forcing her to deep throat all 9 inches of his chocolate stick. As she polished his knob, NOB quickly did the math. As soon as he reached the figure, his nuts swelled and exploded.

"Aghh fuucckkk," he growled as thick, hot nut splashed against the back of her throat. Smacking her lips, Toya raised her head up, proud that she could make him cum so much. Little did she know, the nut had more to do with the potential $400,000 lick than her dick sucking skills.

As the cranberry red Bentley Azure pulled into Ruth's Chris parking lot, Chrissy felt like a queen. Dressed in a black and gold Vera Wang mini dress, with matching knee-high suede and satin boots and a LV clutch. The only one that could compare, would probably be the motherfucker that drove her there.

Decked in a black and gold Versace dress shirt with the Lion head logo as buttons going down the shirt. All black slacks with a pair of black and gold Versace loafers. No chain, just a yellow gold, black diamond Cartier and of course, an enormous and beautiful pinky ring. Every time she looked at him, her pussy lips puckered. She could literally feel her satin thong clinging to her freshly shaved coochie.

As the waiter showed them to their seats, she couldn't help but to acknowledge all the stares from the diners. No doubt, her and Saint looked like a power couple.

With power comes hate. That also was in abundance that night. As their orders were being prepared, Saint gazed into her eyes, attempting to undress her soul.

"What are your plans for the future?" He asked first and foremost. She wanted to tell him about her goal to help Banks get out of jail, but who was she kidding. She hadn't thought about him in the last couple of weeks and hadn't heard from him in almost a year. Her heart tugged at the thought of what might've happened, but she brushed it to the side. She didn't want a sour mood to fuck up her night out with Saint.

"I don't know... I haven't really thought about it," she admitted.

Saint looked at her while caressing her hand. "Look baby girl, life is too short to waste on indecision. I know you may not know where you want to be, but I know where you *don't* want to be. You don't want to be 35 years old, living paycheck to paycheck. Or unemployed, barely making it. Married to someone who's waiting on a chance to upgrade to a better model. I can guarantee in 5 years, you can retire from the streets with your own business. All it takes is loyalty, dedication and obedience. I will teach you how to make money, if you're willing to learn. Just like any other game, there are rules. As long as you follow these rules, you will succeed and *we will* prosper together. You can see it with your own eyes. The proof of everything I'm telling you is real. The cars, the jewels, the homes. All proceeds from good ho'ing and great pimping!"

Chrissy watched and listened in awe, as Saint gave it to her raw and uncut. When he was done, she asked him questions. Of course, he had the correct answer for each one. Once they left the restaurant, he took her to his mini mansion.

As soon as the gates opened up, they were greeted with a fleet of expensive cars. *Does he really own all these cars,* she asked herself as they parked next to a tangerine-colored Lambo.

When she entered the house, she found out exactly who the owners of the cars were. Lined up in formation, were 6 of the most beautiful women Chrissy had ever seen in real life. You had everything from Hawaiian and Dominican mixed, to Bajan with sea green eyes. Chrissy began to feel self-conscious when a Coco look alike approached and introduced herself.

"Heyy, I'm Candy. Welcome to our home. We've heard so much about you." Candy grabbed her hand and led her on tour through the house. She introduced her to all the wife in-laws. Chrissy was thoroughly speechless.

She finally found her voice. "Sooo...Are you the bottom," she meekly asked.

"Me?...Oh no. She's out right now. She'll be back soon though. Her name is Peaches. She's a whole different story, but she's the head wifey, so you know."

After the meet and greet, the girls left Chrissy and Saint for some privacy. Chrissy had made her decision, and she was excited about it. "So, how did you say I choose up again?"

Saint explained that his fee was $30,000. Chrissy almost choked on the wine she was sipping.

"$30,000!"

Saint smiled. He already knew she had the money, because she had confided in Poptart that she had saved up $25,000. Now, it was just a matter of getting her to see why she should invest in his pimping.

"Look my Queen, I know you feel like that's a lot of money, but once I instill this top shelf game into your mainframe, you'll be making $2-$3,000 a night, easily. Plus, everything from this point on is for your retirement plan. At the pace you were going, it would take you forever to reach your goal. I'm about to take you out of that go-cart and put you in a Bugatti."

She took a few seconds to ponder her decision. *Fuck it!* "Aight Daddy...I wanna choose your pimping. I'll have to go back to my house to get the bread I have saved up. I'll be $5,000 short though."

"Well, when it comes to getting paper, we don't use the word short. We consider those installments. He reached out his elbow. She took a hold of it. "Shall we?" As they were walking out, Peaches was walking in.

Peaches was a dime and a half. Mixed with Jamaican and Italian, she had reddish brown hair, golden brown skin, melon sized titties and an ass like Serena Williams. Her skin tone was a shade lighter than Christina Millian. As soon as she saw Saint and Chrissy leaving, her face frowned up. Even though she was the bottom, and it was her duty to welcome in the new wifies, she hated new bitches. Every new bitch was a potential threat in her eyes.

"Uhh..Daddy, are you leaving?" She was hoping to spend some quality time with Saint.

It had been a long time since they had been able to sit back and chill.

"How many times do I have to tell you, stop asking questions you know the answers to. You see I'm exiting my home with my car keys in hand. What, you think I'm 'bout to sit in the car and listen to music," he chastised her.

"You're right Daddy. I apologize," she responded. Already, she had been embarrassed in front of the new girl.

"Oh, where are my manners? Chrissy...This is my Bottom Bitch, Peaches...Peaches, this is the new addition to our family...Chrissy!" The girls shook hands and exchanged pleasantries. Chrissy detected a slight attitude, but she chalked it up to her feeling some type of way about getting checked by Saint. She and Saint departed.

They ended up at the home her and Banks had shared. "Go in and grab everything that belongs to you, because you won't be coming back," he told her as she stepped out of the Bentley.

As she collected her belongings, the memories of her and Banks brought her to tears. Even though she didn't show it when it counted, she really did love him. "I hope you can forgive me boo," she said out loud, as she closed the door *and* that chapter of her life.

Chapter 12

"Yesss. Fuck that pussy. Make it cream daddddyyy!" Tracy laid across the desk in Ant Dawg's office. He pounded her twat, trying to knock the lining out of her pussy. She knew this would be the price for getting back in the game. Banks said, "By any means", and she hoped that he meant that shit. The chick she had given the beat down too, was a main attraction at the club. Plus, her pimp and Ant Dawg had been business associates. When Tracy took her out of the game, she took money out of Ant's pockets.

"Spread that ass open," he commanded. Tracy reached back with both hands, spreading her cheeks apart. She felt an extra inch dig up in her, as her honey dripped and poured out the seams of her sloppy wet pussy.

One thing about Ant, he knew how to fuck a bitch bowlegged. She could feel her nut building up. Climbing up her legs as she was about to explode. "Fuuccckkk...I'm 'bout to cummmm!" She announced.

"Cream on that dick bitch. Cum for Daddy!"

"Oooohh ssshhiiittt. I'm cumming... I'm cummmiinngg!" With wave after wave, her nut squirted everywhere. Over a year of built-up frustration was released onto Ant Dawg's dick. She wanted Banks to be the one to uncork her cunt, but Ant made a great substitute.

As her body laid on the desk convulsing, her pussy spasmed and proved to be too much for him. "Aghh shit. Here it cums...Fuck! Here it cums, Sparkle!" She jumped up, grabbed his dick and jacked him off until he nutted all over her face. Ant looked down at her messy features. "Damn girl, you haven't lost it. You're hired... *Again!*" They both began to laugh at that.

Of course, if she wanted to become the top bitch in the club, fucking Ant would become a regular thing. Being the top bitch meant being on stage at prime time. That's when all the big spenders come out. She would be the first and sometimes the only girl sent to VIP. So, letting Ant dig up in her coochie from time to time, wasn't a bad trade off.

After she cleaned herself off, she made her way back to the locker room. She wasn't looking forward to fraternizing with them stank ass hoes, but hey. That was part of the job.

"Hey girl...I heard you were back. I ain't believe it, but here you are in the flesh," a redbone stripper by the name of Passion greeted her.

"Yeah girl...You know a bitch can't stay gone for too long," Tracy replied.

"Naw...What it is, is your stank ass ran out of money, so you came back. Ready to suck Ant's dick to let you dance," a familiar voice spat. They both turned to see Diamond and her flunky Ruby standing by the doorway. Both of them were part of Cream's old crew. Diamond looked just like Lisa Raye from the movie Playa's Club, and Ruby looked like a knock off version of her cousin Ebony.

Apparently they were still feeling some type of way about what happened to their homegirl. Even so, they were wise enough not to step to Tracy head on.

"Naw bitch, you just wish all that dick Ant lets you suck would have you dancing at prime time instead of turning tricks for peanuts like the elephant that you are. You hoes kill me. Y'all will suck a nigga dick for a blunt, then let him blow your twat out for a cheeseburger. Bitch, step your game up! Maybe if you wasn't hating on a real bitch so much, you could take notes and upgrade that 15 year old Honda you got," Tracy capped.

"Bitch! Whatever. You ain't shit," Diamond spat as she stomped out of the locker room.

Passion giggled. Tracy looked at her with raised eyebrows.

"What's so funny?"

"Nothing girl... Welcome back," she laughed while finishing her makeup.

Tracy pulled out her red, one-piece slingshot with her 4-inch stilettos. With her makeup flawless, she hit the floor. *Damn it's been a minute.* The club was packed. She made her way to the bar. "Give me a shot of Patron, Kim."

"Oh heyy girl, I got you. One shot of Patron coming right up," Kim the bartender said before moving to the next customer. As Tracy surveyed the club, she caught a fine ass brother staring her down. She sashayed over to his area to get a better appraisal. She checked out his shoes. Maury Gators, Robin Jeans and a few stones in his ear and watch. *He might be worth a few minutes,* she surmised.

"Heyy sexy. You wanna dance," she purred.

"Uhh...Sure!" She sat in his lap and dirty wined onto his rising erection. She felt his rod stiffening, so she maneuvered so it would lay nestled between her ass cheeks. She definitely knew how to seduce.

She let him feel her up, but not too much. She even let him diddle her clit, but she wouldn't allow him to put his fingers in her pussy. By the end of the third song, he had a raging hard on, and was in desperate need of release. "How much," he whispered in her ear as she continued to wind on him.

"$200 for the top, $400 for bottom...$500 for both," she whispered back.

"I just want some pussy."

"Well, that's gonna be $400." He reached into his pocket and pulled out four crisp hundred dollar bills. Tracy took them and stuffed them in her money bag she kept tied to her wrist.

She stood up and allowed him to slip his condom on. With his dick sticking straight up, she grabbed and positioned it as she slid down. He looked to be about 6 inches, but this was about business and not pleasure.

She worked the dick like a 9 to 5. Popping her pussy and gripping his cock, until he exploded into the condom. The whole time it appeared as though she was just giving a routine lap dance.

Once he came, she hopped off $400 richer. They exchanged numbers and she headed to the back for a quick shower. *Tonight will be a good night,* she told herself as she headed back onto the dance floor.

Bam pulled up to the agreed upon location. A dead-end street in 5th Ward. He had a bad feeling in his gut. He tried to tell himself he was just nervous because this was his first major drug buy, but he couldn't shake the feeling. He had met Toya's cousin a few times and the nigga seemed legit, but now that he was in the middle of the ghetto, with $400,000 of someone else's money, he couldn't help but to be worried.

Before he left the crib, he had Toya call her cousin. He said he would be waiting. *So where the fuck is he?* As he picked his phone up and was about to call, he spotted a black Charger in some 22" Lexanis. *Finally!*

Ron, better known as NOB, hopped out his front seat and made his way over to Bam's money green 745 LI., with a duffle bag. Bam nervously checked his side and rearview mirrors as Ron slid into his passenger seat.

What's crackin Cuz," Ron said. Extending the "C" so Bam could lock up.

Bam reached into the backseat, grabbed the duffle bag and handed it over. Ron inspected it, then handed him the duffle bag full of dope. Bam grabbed it, opened it up and looked inside. His eyes became buck. Inside the bag was a bunch of cement bricks, with red bandanas tied around them. *What the fuck!*

When he whipped his head up, he was staring down the barrel of a nickel plated .357. Instantly Bam's heart dropped.

"Come on Ron, don't do the game like this. I'm fucking with your cousin the long way," Bam pleaded.

"Ain't nothing personal nigga, this is all bidness," NOB spat.

"Come on, Cuz. I'm about to marry your cousin. We practically family!" Bam whined.

"Cuz?...Cuz! Bitch ass nigga. This Blood Game. Woo Wooo. As far as Toya, or should I say Stacy." NOB pulled out his phone and pressed play on a video of Toya giving him sloppy head while he drove. "That's my bitch nigga!" With that, NOB pulled the trigger.

BOCKA!

Bam's head shaped sideways. His brains flew through the shattered driver's side window. NOB's right-hand man Marlo hopped out the Charger with a can full of gasoline. Once the Beamer was thoroughly doused, they stepped back and threw the match. *Whoooooossshh!* As Bam and the car went up in flames, they jumped in the Charger and sped off.

Bam was 3 hours late and he still hadn't answered his phone. Paccy couldn't stop pacing. *This nigga better not have tried to play me.* He knew deep down, he should've never let the nigga quarterback the play. He dialed his number for the 50th time...No answer!

Just as he was about to throw his phone at the wall, he caught something on TV. The volume was on mute, but the screen flashed...*Breaking News!* He unmuted the TV and listened to the reporter *"Police were called to a scene where a vehicle was apparently burning. Inside, was an unidentified body believed to be a male. No ID was recovered, and police are asking anyone with information to please come forward."*

Paccy recognized the Beamer. He knew immediately it was Bam. "FUCK!" he screamed at the top of his lungs. "They jacked the lil' homie, with all my fucking bread!" He screamed at no one in particular. Now, he was back to being dead broke. Now, it was back to what he knew best.

Dorian wasn't too sure what was wrong with Paccy, but she knew whatever it was, it was really bothering him. He would barely speak to her. Word on the street, Dread was dead. She always felt that would make her feel better. On the contrary, she felt worse. She was scared to death that Paccy would find out it was her who set Dread up.

Everyone was walking on eggshells. The only good thing was, he was barely home these days. It was also a bad thing, because she didn't know what was on his mind. Today was one of those rare days where he was home and she decided to feel him out a bit. Paccy sat on the couch with a scowl on his face. Apparently, in deep thought. Dorian approached him timidly.

"Heyy boo. Would you like for me to cook you something to eat?"

"Naw, I'm good, D." She could feel the ice dripping off his words. She tried a different approach. She sat next to him, reaching for his belt buckle. Paccy pushed her hand away. "I'm good, D!"

She couldn't believe it. It'd been almost a week since he laid a finger on her. *What the fuck is going on,* she wondered. "Well babe, I'm 'bout to hit the mall. Can I have some money? I saw this new St. Laurent I wanted."

Paccy's face twitched. He wanted to lie, but at the end of the day, it was no use. You can't hide the fact you're broke. The few bands he had left were barely enough for the bills for the next couple months. He looked Dorian in the eyes. He wasn't sure if she would continue to ride it out once she realized he was broke.

"Look baby, Bam got smoked a few days ago. I sent him on a buy with everything I had left. The nigga he was dealing with robbed, killed and smoked him. *Literally!* I don't have a pot to piss in. My connect is in the Feds and most likely down for the count."

Dorian listened to him pour his soul out. She knew what it meant for a nigga like Paccy to admit the things he was admitting to her. She couldn't believe, just last month they were on top of the world. Now, they were penniless.

Even though the money is what attracted her to him, she grew to fall in love with Paccy. She was willing to ride it out with him, as well as do what was necessary to see him rise back to the top. She knew at that exact moment, he needed to hear her tell him that.

"Boo, I know you're not 'bout to let that shit break you. You've been at the bottom before and you're headed to the top again. Regardless, I'm not going anywhere. I got you no matter what. Win, lose or draw. Your queen is in your corner." For the first time in days, she saw a smile on her man's face.

Paccy grabbed her chin, lifted it up and looked her dead in her eyes. "Real shit D, I didn't expect for a nigga to fall for you, but I have. I apologize for putting us in this position. For trusting snakes and not being the G, I was bred to be. On my life, my set and everything I hold dear I'm not going to stop until we get to the top. I love you for real girl, and I'll lay a nigga down behind you!"

"Aww, I love you too baby," Dorian cooed. Paccy embraced her into a passionate kiss. For the first time since they started messing with each other, they made love until the early morning.

While Dorian slept, exhausted from the 5 orgasms she had, Paccy sat in bed, formulating his plan for the comeback. He knew he wasn't equipped to go after Pierre, who he thought was responsible for robbing and killing his lil' homie. Little did he know, the real Pierre had no idea who Bam or Paccy was. Much less, what had transpired.

Paccy needed to get his chips up before he went to war. As he watched her sleep, he knew what needed to be done. He just hoped she meant those words, because he was sure about to test her dedication.

It's been weeks since Tracy started stripping. Banks could tell by her demeanor at work. Her body language was slow and lethargic. He would often catch her napping in the picket. Then, when he tried to call her after work, she would often be too tired to talk and would complain about needing to get some rest so she could hit up the club. He couldn't trip. After all, this was his idea. He gave her the space she needed.

She did it solely for him, so he had to try and minimize her stress as much as possible. As he and Serve sat in his cell eating homemade enchiladas, courtesy of Tracy, a new house entered. A new house meant a new inmate and due to the standing beef between the South and the East, every inmate was subject to questioning.

"Where you from homie," an inmate named Buck asked the new house.

"I'm East Side, One Trey Seven," he replied proudly.

"Oh yeah? Well one of your homies is upstairs," Buck informed him.

"Who's dat?"

"Bankroll."

"What? Banks is here? Where he at," the new house frantically asked. Obviously excited about being on the same tank as Banks. Buck escorted him to Bank's cell and made the introductions. As soon as Banks saw the lil' homie, his face lit up.

He hadn't seen lil' Orin in a minute. Lil' Orin was always a lil' hard headed, but he was a bonafide hustler. He used to grab his work from Banks and hit the small towns on the outskirts of Houston. Crosby, Aimes, Barrett Station, Conroe, etc. His name had been booming for a minute. He was sure to be a candidate for the next "King of the City!"

"Aww shit. What it is, Big Blood?!" Tyler locked up and hugged his big homie.

"Damn O, what's it been? 'bout two years since I seen you?"

"Yeah Blood, something like that. You know a nigga been tryna stack my bread up. I heard 'bout that bogus murder case they put on you."

"That ain't shit to a steppa. I'm 'bout to beat that bitch," Banks assured him.

"I heard 'bout Killa too. That's fucked up. I'd have never thought a nigga could have caught *him* slipping," Orin explained.

At hearing the mention of his bro's name, Banks couldn't do much but nod solemnly. "What they got you for this time," Banks asked.

"Aww shit, I got a bullshit ass pistol case. They caught me coming out of the Glen."

"The Glen? Nigga, what was you doing over there?"

"Mann Blood, I was fucking with this lil' bitch named Salena. I had already got into with her brother and his faggot ass homeboys. Ain't no way I was sliding in and out that bitch without my pole."

"That's ovastood. Better to get caught with it, than without it," Banks preached. "You still smoke?"

"Hell yeah I still smoke," Orin declared.

"Well I got some Diesel left. You can twist and burn one with us. Oh, my bad. Serve, this one of my lil' homies from the block, Orin. Orin, this *my* big homie aka Boss Playa Serve."

Serve and Orin dabbed each other up. Orin twisted up a blunt and they blew until they were all slant eyed. "Get ready for count!" Tracy announced over the intercom. Once they were all lined up and counted, Orin couldn't wait to get back in the cell.

"Say B, I know that bitch," Orin said excitedly.

"Who? Officer Jones?" Banks attention was definitely piqued.

"Yeah...I wasn't sure when I got my housing card, but now that I see her up close...Yeah that's her!"

"Where you know her from," Banks hesitantly asked.

"Shit... I just buss that hoe pussy open the other night at the club. I ain't gone lie, a nigga paid $500, but that head and pussy was well worth it. She even let me pull out and buss on her face. I'm telling you Blood, she a freak for real!" Orin sounded as if he'd fucked Halle Berry, the way he was carrying on.

After hearing Orin's revelation, Serve paid close attention to Banks. This was the first test. To see if he was truly ready for the game. Could Banks handle his woman doing what it took? Even if it meant she was sucking dick and fucking tricks?

Sensing Serve's eyes appraising him, Banks kept his composure. Truthfully, he was crushed inside. Mainly because, Tracy insisted that she only danced and wasn't turning tricks. Plus, he hadn't even sampled the goods yet. Still, he had to remember. In this game, profit comes before pussy. Sometimes a P will have a hoe he will never get to pop.

Serve had warned him that she may be hesitant to disclose what was really going on, because their relationship began square. She feared it would be too much too soon and Banks wouldn't be able to handle it. He looked at Orin. "Oh yeah? She got some good like that?"

"What? Hell yeah. I'm talking some of the best I ever had," Orin boasted.

"That's wassup. I wonder if she'd do a nigga's welcome home party," Banks replied as he finished off the Dro stick. He had to admit to himself, he definitely had to straighten her out. He was taught, if you'll lie, you'll steal and if you'll steal, you deserve to be killed. For the last few weeks, she had been lying to him. He was smart enough to know, he couldn't let his emotions dictate his moves. In the grand scheme of things, she was only doing what she was supposed to do. Hoe to the best of her abilities. Later that night, Banks hit her cell.

"Heyyy, Daddy!"

"What's up, my Queen?"

"Just tired as hell. Working both jobs, but a bitch gotta do what she gotta do to bring her King home." That definitely brought a smile to his face. After giving it some thought, he decides to use reverse psychology.

"Say boo, I got a suggestion for you."

"Wassup? What you got on your mind," she asked sort of wearily.

"Well, you been having some really good nights at the club, but I feel you could double or even triple it, if you gave them trick ass niggas what they really want.

"And what's that," she asked curiously.

"Instead of counting 20's at a time for lap dances, you should start popping them for a stack or better for the real deal."

Tracy became silent. Banks already knew she was charging $500. Now, she felt like she had to step it up, because *now* he was asking her to turn tricks. Which she had already been doing, but he didn't know that. Or so she thought.

"So you want me to start turning tricks," she asked incredulously.

"Yeah, I mean, if we gone do this, we might as well do it the right way. No half stepping, full stride! I know your love for me is indestructible, and so is mine for you. I just feel like, if you're making $800- $1,200 a night just lap dancing, imagine what you could make if you start turning tricks. He used her lie to back her into a corner. If she accepted, she had no choice but to turn all the way up. How could she explain that she made more giving lap dances, than she did turning tricks. She couldn't!

Of course Tracy agreed and Banks never let on that he already knew she was selling pussy. Serve sat in his cell next to him and listened to his young apprentice "work". *Now, that's what you call pimping!*

Chapter 13

Chrissy and Peaches had just landed in Atlanta. She'd been down with Saint for close to a month and a half by now. He felt like Chrissy was ready for some cross-country ho'ing. What better bitch to send with her, than his bottom bitch, Peaches. They were to spend 3 weeks in Atlanta, 3 weeks in Miami, then 3 weeks in New York.

While they were on tour, they were required to deposit money in different accounts at several local banks in the area, and Saint would have one of his other hoes withdraw the money back in Texas. Peaches was known to pull at least $50,000 in every city she visited. That meant by the end of her nine-week tour, she'd have over a 150k.

Chrissy knew Peaches was one of, if not the baddest bitches in the game. If she planned on replacing her, which she did, she had to find a way to out trap her. Even though they kept their relationship cordial, and somewhat friendly, at the end of the day, it was every bitch for themselves.

From the research they conducted, they knew Gucci Mane and Rick Ross were going to be in Magic City the night they landed. Due to Saints connects, and an undisclosed amount that was wired to the owner and manager, Chrissy and Peaches were on their roster for the next 30 days.

As they checked into the Hilton suite, they couldn't help but notice all the stares. Saint had taught them, getting money started when you get out of bed in the morning. The way you look will determine if you hook a whale before your set for *sale*!

Chrissy pulled out her black and red pleated skirt, with a white button blouse, making sure to show ample cleavage. With no bra to hold them still, white 4-inch pumps, she looked like Sarah Palin on the way to audition for a porno.

Peaches jumped out with a spray-painted wife beater. No bra, nipples poking like a set of '84 swangers. She kept it sporty with gray and white Dunks. Even though they were dressed as polar opposites, one thing for sure. They were two of the baddest women in the city, and they planned on letting everyone know before the 3 weeks were up.

After picking up their rental car, they made their way up to the infamous strip club. As usual, it was packed. And they were early! They called Saint to let him know they were pulling up. He called the manager.

Once inside, they were shown to their lockers. "Girrrlll..Did you see that crowd," Chrissy sang out. This was her first time in the A. Shit, this was her first time out of Texas.

Peaches was no stranger to Magic City. Or any of the major clubs in the country for that matter!

She tolerated Chrissy's enthusiasm. She remembered how it was when she first started. How excited she was to see the world for the first time.

"Yeah girl, it's gonna be one of those nights. I seen them Maybach Music niggas in the place, and if I ain't tripping, I think I seen Plies just walk in.

Chrissy looked at Peaches and asked, " What you think you'll be able to pull tonight?"

Peaces already knew where her mind was at. She welcomed the challenge. "Shit... At least $2,500-$3,000."

"Well, let's make a bet. The bitch with the best trap, the other buys lunch tomorrow," Chrissy proposed.

Peaches couldn't contain her smile. *What makes this bitch think she could even lick my stilettos. She just got down 2 months ago, and she already tryna buck a Boss Bitch!* She smirked and replied, "That's a bet!" With that, they both finished getting dressed and headed to the dance floor.

Smack!

"That's right bitch...Take this dick!"

Smack!

Troy couldn't get enough of this thick ass caramel. He smacked her repeatedly on the ass and watched her Straight Stunna booty jiggle and shake. She looked back at him, daring him to go even deeper.

"Oohh...Fuck this pussy nigga...Buss it open, baby!"

Troy couldn't take anymore.

"I'm 'bout to cum... Agghh shit fucckk!" She hopped off his dick and got in position. He snatched the condom off and held his dick over her opened mouth. Hot sticky cum shot out his piss hole, filling her mouth to the brim. She squeezed and squeezed, until every drop was licked and sucked clean. Then, gave his nuts a tongue bath. Just in case, any of his cum spilled onto them. Dick still twitching, Troy collapsed on the King size bed.

He'd been seeing Rachel for the last 3 months and it always seemed as if she'd gotten better. After much persistence on her part, he finally gave her the title of wifey. Now, they were both laid up at his 5-bedroom home in Sugarland, right on the outskirts of Houston. "Damn girl...The pussy is out of control good," he panted, clearly out of breath. "You make a nigga wanna put a ring on it for real."

She chuckled. "Oh yeah?"

"Hell yeah!"

She grabbed his limp dick and started to play with it. Even though he'd came twice already, it still began to rise to her touch. "Baby...I wanna go shopping tomorrow. It's my brother's birthday. Could you give me some money pleeeaassee," she pouted.

"Yeah boo, I got you. How much you need?"

142

"Just a couple stacks...Oh wait, we gotta wait for the banks to open up, huh?"

"Naw...I got some bread in my safe over here. I don't really fuck with banks. I got you."

Hearing that, she stuffed his rod back in her mouth. She sucked and slurped until he passed out. Then she got up to use the restroom.

30 minutes later, as Troy laid peacefully sleeping, 2 men crept into his home. As he dreamt of walking on a sandy beach with Rachel, a sharp, excruciating pain shot through the side of his face.

WHAP!

Oh shit... What the fuck?! For a second, he didn't know what was going on until his vision cleared and seen two men he'd never seen before, standing at the edge of his bed. Guns pointed at him and Rachel. *Wait. Where is Rachel?"* Rachel was gone!

What he didn't know was, Rachel wasn't her real name... Dorian was. And one of the men standing at the edge of his bed, was none other than the leader of the IGF, OG Paccy! If he knew who he was looking at, Troy would've realized his chances of survival were slim to none.

Troy was a mid-level coke dealer, who happened to have a tender dick. When he met *Rachel* at his homeboy's birthday bash 3 months ago, he felt he had to have her. After he took her home, he blew her back out. Then, she blew his mind. He couldn't get enough of her. Until 2 nights ago, he'd never brought her to where he laid his head. Now that he had, she verified it was where he kept the bulk of his bread. She sicked the wolves on him.

Paccy grabbed the back of his head and pushed him off the bed. "Where the safe at nigga?"

Come on man...Pleeasee don't do this," Troy begged with tears in his eyes.

BOCKA!

"Agghhh shit. Man, my shoulder!" He screamed as blood gushed from the wound in his right shoulder.

"I'm not gonna ask again!"

"Aight... Aight...Hold on man. I got you. Just please don't kill me," Troy pleaded. Troy crawled into his walk-in closet and removed a false panel, revealing a safe. His hands trembled as he inserted the combination. The electronic safe beeped twice.

Beep. Beep. The light turned green. As soon as the safe door was open and Paccy saw all those stacks of money, he aimed his .40 at the back of Troy's head and squeezed.

BOCKA!

Troy's head snapped forward. His face collided with the safe. Pieces of his brains and skull were on the money, but Paccy could give a fuck less. He began to stuff the bills into the black trash bags.

"J-Bang...Sweep for jewelry, I'll grab the bedsheets!" He didn't need any of Dorian's DNA on the scene. Once they grabbed all the valuable possessions, they doused the house with gasoline. Then, set it ablaze.

Waiting in the getaway car was Dorian. "Go! Go! Go! Go!" Paccy urged as the 3 pulled off into the night. This was Dorian's fourth lick she'd set them on.

At first, she didn't think she could do it. Now, she felt as though she was born to do it. Her knack for spotting good licks was getting good. Her first two were only $22,000 and $34,000 respectfully. The third was $56,000. She couldn't wait to see what was this one brought in.

After discarding the dope fiend rental, they returned back to the condo. They discovered Troy was doing alright for himself. $143,000 with jewelry wasn't a bad take. After giving J-Bang his cut, Dorian and Paccy hopped in the shower together. It's something about hitting a lick, that always got her pussy wet as hell.

While the water sprayed against his back, she dropped to a squat and stuffed her mouth full of cock. She relaxed her throat to allow all his length to fit snug. With her tongue, she flicked the tip against his balls, while humming around his shaft.

Paccy grabbed the back of her head with 2 hands, long stroking the inside of her jaws. Before long, his balls started to twitch. He gritted his teeth and nutted on her tongue. She swallowed but refused to let up. His knees buckled as he tried to pry her off his dick. She locked on like a vicious pit bull. She sucked and slurped until he came for a second time. Back to back. After they got out the shower, they continued their session until they passed out in each other's arms.

After lunch at Justin's, courtesy of Chrissy, her and Peaches set off to deposit their traps into the designated bank accounts. Chrissy still couldn't believe Peaches had outdid her the previous night. Chrissy made $4,840. She thought for sure that would be the high total. Until Peaches announced she pulled in $5,080. Chrissy watched as Peaches recounted in front of her, just to make sure.

Peaches couldn't help but throw a quick verbal jab. "Come on C, you really thought your rookie ass could out hoe me. I've been ho'ing since I was 15. You've got a lot of ground to cover in them stilettos, if you tryna to get a Boss Bitch's trap," she bragged.

What Chrissy didn't know was Peaches only eclipsed her total by stealing out of another stripper's purse. Lucky for her, the girl had $800. That put Peaches over Chrissy by a couple hundred. She knew by how the night started, she was going to have to pull something off, because Chrissy had been on fire.

"Okay bitch...You act like you beat me by a stack or better. If we had 30 more minutes to work clean, lunch would have been on you," she joked. Chrissy respected Peaches ho'ing , but she also felt like she was mostly hype, and could muscle in on her position in due time.

We need to go ahead and get out of here. I need to get ready for one of my clients, "Peaches said as she made her way to the front door. Chrissy paid the tab, but as she was getting up to leave, she locked eyes with a sexy ass brother sitting with a female.

It was difficult to tell how tall he was, but his money definitely was "ball player" tall. From the looks of things, the female with him appeared to be his girlfriend. Chrissy could give 2 fucks if it was. She was new in Atlanta and didn't have any high-end clientele. This could very well be one.

She seductively licks her lips and makes it as if she forgot something. Heading instead, to the restroom. Chrissy already knew from his vantage point, he had a direct line of sight to the bathrooms. She waited until he glanced in her direction.

Within seconds, he searched for her. They locked eyes. Chrissy curled her finger, giving him the "come here" signal, before she continued into the bathroom. After about 45 seconds of idle waiting, her admirer decided to excuse himself from his table, and headed her way.

His date, who was completely unaware of the exchange, simply said, "Okay babe". She watched as he walked away. His heart thumped in his chest. The prospect of him getting some fresh pussy while his girl waited, excited him to no end.

Ever since he'd seen Peaches and Chrissy walk in, he couldn't stop stealing glances. Even with his girl Tara there, he just couldn't help it. He secretly told himself, he would gladly eat either one of their assholes out if they gave him the chance.

"Pssst...Over here." Chrissy was in one of the stalls waiting on him. With a huge grin on his face, he walked over to her. As he stepped into the stall, his hard-on bumped into her stomach. She looked up into his eyes as she massaged his dick through his jeans. She put the toilet seat down, sat on it, then rubbed over his print. "What's your name, handsome?"

"Uhh shit...My name's Sache," he stuttered out, overwhelmed by the sensual massage she was administering.

Chrissy wet her bottom lip. "Is that your girlfriend out there," she asked as she unzipped his jeans and fished out his rod. You could see the relief in his eyes as her warm hands stroked his meat.

"Sssshh...Yeahhh...Tha... That's my girl," he admitted.

"Well look baby, I don't give a damn if she is. I'll give you my number so you can call me up later and we can discuss some things...Aight?" Chrissy picked up the pace, stroking him with quickness. All he could do was nod his head as she reached in his pocket and grabbed his phone. With her left hand on his dick and the right hand on his phone, she inserted her number and saved it. She dialed her number, and waited for *her* phone to ring. Now, she had his.

His dick began to twitch. She felt he was about to cum, so she stopped and placed his brick hard cock back in his boxers. The look of wanting, lust and disappointment was plastered all over Sache's face. She patted his crotch twice, then stood up. "Call me later, so we can discuss how to finish this up," she whispered in his ear. "I hope your girl leaves some nut for me, because a bitch's thirsty as hell."

As she walked out the restroom, she eyed Sache's girl waiting patiently. A small smirk graced Chrissy's lips. She didn't know the woman, so she didn't feel any type of way. At the end of the day, business is business. And Chrissy is always about hers.

When she finally did make it back to the car, Peaches gave her an earful. "Damn hoe. What took you so long. I told you I had a client waiting. Let me find out you trynna block a bitch bag!"

Chrissy looked at her annoyed. "Girl please, I ain't trynna hate on your shit. I had a potential client I needed to reel in real quick. If your trick can't wait a few extra minutes, then you ain't putting it down right. I know all mine will wait 'til the end of time for this great neck and this wet wet."

Peaches couldn't help but to smile at that. "Yeah... Yeah...Whatever bitch!" She put the rental car in gear and pulled out of the parking lot.

Sache returned to his table after having to jack his dick just to relieve himself of the pressure Chrissy left on his dick and balls. He looked in his contacts and noticed she saved her number under Jewelz. Now, he knew her name. As he sat listening to his girl Tara talk his ear off about the job, all he could think about was fucking Jewelz later that night.

As Chrissy and Peaches got ready for their second night at Magic City, she wondered how much bread Sache was playing with. By the way he was acting when she had him hemmed up in the stall, she knew she'd be able to bleed him dry. She just had to figure out, will it be short term or long term?

"Say C, have you seen my Dior shades," Peaches asked, interrupting her thoughts. Chrissy looked up and saw Peaches standing in the doorway in nothing but some pink silk panties. Her titties hung freely. Chrissy wasn't gay. Well, not all the way. Really, she was a little confused every now and then, but she had to admit, Peaches was a very sexy woman.

"Naw...I hadn't seen them. Wait. As a matter of fact, I think I did see them. I found them under the bed, so I put them in my closet." Peaches left to retrieve her shades, while Chrissy continued her train of thought. Suddenly, her phone rang. Nikki Minaj's "I'm a Bad Bitch," belted from the headset. She looked at the screen and smiled. *Sache!*

"Hello?"

"Is this Jewelz?

"Of course it is. Who else would it be?"

"Well, I'm trynna see what you had planned for tonight. You know you left a nigga on stuck. Blue balls and all.

"Poor baby. Mama had your nuts hurting," she cooed.

"Oh, you got jokes huh? Hell yeah a nigga nuts was hurting. I'm saying. Are you gone finish what you started, or was that all cap?"

"Well...I gotta work tonight. I won't get off until 4-5 in the morning. If you want, you can come up to my job. When I'm done, we can leave together."

"That sounds cool with me. Where you work at," he asked.

"Magic City."

"Oh yeah? Well let me know when you get there. Me and my niggas will fall off in the section."

"Will y'all be in VIP," she asked, hoping they were. If they weren't, that would say a lot about their paper.

"Hell yeah...Ain't no other way. We usually try to have the whole VIP on lock!" Chrissy smiled at that. *Jackpot!,* she thought as she wrapped up the conversation. "Well boo...I'll see you tonight then."

"Bet," he said before he hung up. Chrissy had to pat herself on the back. Because she had been assertive, she had a potential long-term trick in her pocket. At the very least, she should make a bankroll at work. She slipped on her Fendi skirt and top, sprayed on her Chanel, and they made their way out the door.

The club wasn't as packed as it was the previous night. Still, it was a lot of money to be made. Chrissy, Peaches, along with 4 other strippers, had gotten chosen to work VIP for Sache and his crew. It turned out, Sache was a major player in the game. His mom was half Mexican on her dad's side of the family, and was linked to the Sinaloa cartel.

Even though they weren't too fond of interracial marriages, or even interracial kids for that matter, Sache's family supported him, and respected his hustle. Through them, he was able to lock down Atlanta with cocaine and meth. He had assembled a team of hitters, called the Big Bag Cartel or the BBC!

The BBC was in full effect that night. Bottles were being bought and poured out like they were water. Thousands of dollars rained all night in VIP until the floor was completely covered in green backs. Regardless of his spending habits, Sache didn't dress flashy. You could still tell he was a Boss nigga. Dressed in a simple Polo shirt and 501 jeans, he sat while Chrissy went to work on his hips.

She already told the girls on duty, Sache belonged to her. He was off limits. Every lap dance went to her. She knew she had him when she felt his hard dick poking through the denim of his jeans. She let him caress her clit, while she danced and moaned into his ear. She glanced to her right. Peaches was doing her best shit on one of Sache's homeboys. She was making her ass clap in his face.

"Smack that ass, baby boy," she told him as her booty jiggled and wobbled to and fro.

Chrissy knew it was going to be a good night. When she was done with her lap dance, she let Sache know she would only be in town for a couple weeks. She claimed she was grinding for her little brother's surgery.

She really didn't know if he believed her or not, but it really didn't matter. For one, he couldn't prove it and two, by the time she put that head and pussy on him, he would be hooked anyway. She went on to explain how she was really feeling him and how she hated that she had to strip to be able to take care of the things she needed. Sache told her he understood, and didn't mind giving her money. He respected her grind. He felt like strippers were female D Boys. So from one hustler to another, it was all love.

They agreed on $2,500 for the night. Add that to the $840 she has made thus far, not bad for a slow night. She looked for Peaches and spotted her between 2 niggas. She was talking to both, simultaneously. She knew Peaches would be in either one, or both of their pockets by the end of the night.

She caught her attention to let her know she needed to talk to her. As they made their way to the restroom, Chrissy laced her up on her plans for the night. "I'm 'bout to bounce with Sache. I'ma text you and let you know what room we'll be at. What you got up?"

"I don't know yet. Them 2 niggas talking 'bout they want a double up. I told them I'd do it for $1,500 a piece, but they talking 'bout they only trynna spend 2 bands total. So, I don't know. I really ain't tryna low ball. But if nothing else better shake, a bitch gone have to go ahead and hit that," Peaches confessed.

"Okay. Well take the car. I'ma spend the night with Sache. I'ma see if I can get a lil' more out his ass in the morning," Chrissy said while watching Sache as he watched her.

"Aight, well don't forget to text me when you get to the room, and I'll do the same."

"Fa Sho! And girl be careful!"

"You too," Peaches replied as they made their way back to VIP. After a few more minutes, everyone began to break away. Each crew member, snatching up a stripper to bring back to the room with them.

As Sache and Chrissy pulled up to the Marriott, she noticed the Charger she and Peaches rented, turning into the same parking lot. Right behind her was a Black Escalade and a Yukon Denali. *Peaches must have scored both for the night.* A few moments later, her phone vibrated with a text.

Peaches: I'm at Marriott. I'll hit u wit the room # soon.

Chrissy dialed Peaches number. "Hello," Peaches answered.

"I just got your message. I'm at the Marriott too. I think I just saw your ass. Where you at?"

"What? Where *you* at?"

"I'm looking at you bitch," Chrissy couldn't stop laughing. Peaches kept moving her head back and forth on a swivel, like someone just told her the Feds were coming. No doubt, she was looking for some type of big body foreign, but Sache drove a late model MKZ. "I'm over here in the Lincoln."

"Aww shit. Bitch, I was looking everywhere for your ass!" They both began to laugh. Sache walked out of the hotel lobby, headed back to the car.

"Room 282," he told Chrissy as he popped the trunk to grab her overnight bag.

"Girl I'm in 282," she told Peaches as she watched one of her tricks approach the driver side door to let her know what room they were in.

"Well, I'm in room 318," Peaches told her as they wished each other luck, before hanging up.

Once inside the room, Chrissy told Sache she needed a shower to get cleaned first. When she came out of the bathroom dripping wet, Sache took one look at her and couldn't contain himself any longer. He slipped her right breast into his mouth as he gently began to suck on her nipple.

Chrissy moaned as she grabbed a hold of his dick with her right hand, stroking it back and forth. She pushed him down onto the bed and crawled until she was eye level with his rod. Pre cum oozed from the tip. She dabbed it up with her tongue. A soft moan escaped his lip.

She spit on his cock, massaging and coating his shaft with her saliva. She fondled his balls with her left hand, as she slid his length deep down her throat.

He grabbed ahold of her head, pulled her into him, while attempting to make her gag. She knew the first impression was the best impression. She knew she needed to show him how a Boss Bitch took that dick. She bobbed her head and worked his stick to perfection. "Glulp...Glulp...Glup." Chrissy felt his balls draw up, and knew he was about to explode.

"Ooh shit, Jewelz!. You 'bout to make a nigga nut... Fuucckk!" Chrissy took the dick out of her mouth.

"Give me that nut baby...Cum all on my pretty face."

Sache grabbed ahold of the sheets. His toes curled. He screamed out, "Awww fuuccckkk!"

Nut shot from his dick and painted Chrissy's face white.

"Damn!...You a fool on that dick," Sache declared. Clearly winded.

"Now it's time for you to taste momma's pussy. Let me skeet on your lips," she said as they exchanged positions. Sache loved a woman who was aggressive, and Chrissy was turning him on. His girl Tara was always waiting on him to give instructions when fucking. He loved a woman who was assertive. If you want the dick, come *take* it.

Chrissy rode his face until she splashed honeydew all over his lips and chin. They both realized they were in for a long, wonderful night.

Meanwhile, in room 318, Peaches had 8 inches of cock crammed into her mouth, while 9 inches of hard dick sawed into her twat. Roc was the 8 inches and Chris was the 9. Chris spread her fluffy cheeks apart, spit in her pinkish brown asshole while he continued to drill her from the back.

'Clap! Clap! Clap! Clap!' Her ass cheeks crashed against his abs. Roc urged her on.

"Yeeeaahh..Take that dick you nasty bitch."

Peaches took it all like a champ. Spit and precum dripped out of her mouth, as Roc's balls slapped wildly against her chin. Truth be told, Peaches was one of the few hoes that actually enjoyed the sexual acts. Her motto was, the bigger the better. When Roc pulled out of her mouth, she had time to scream. "My ass! Put it in my ass!"

Happy to oblige, Roc positioned himself behind her. With the help of a lot of spit and pussy juice, he slid into her round tight poop shoot.

"Oohh fuck!...I feel so full," Peaches screamed as the sensation of being double penetrated took her into ecstasy. She came within minutes.

The original plan was to pay for only an hour, but after the men felt how good her pussy was, they agreed to both pay her an extra $500 to fuck all night. Altogether she made $3,000 off them and an extra $960 from the club. She wasn't sure what Chrissy made, but she knew Daddy was going to be happy in the morning.

Chapter 14

Finally, the day came when the District Attorney had to dismiss all the chargers. The State's witness still hadn't surfaced, and Joe convinced the D.A. and the judge that the State would be wasting valuable taxpayers dollars, if they took Brandon to trial. Basically, they either had to shit or get off the pot.

On his way back from court, all he could do was smile. Especially, when Tracy came to work. *She* made it happen. She went beyond the call of duty. As soon as she saw the smile on his face, she knew her King was coming home.

They'd agreed, she'd quit the day he was released. It's not that she hated her job. Now the Banks was coming home, she didn't see any point in maintaining it. Her paychecks were about $900 a week. Shit, she made that and more, in one night at Bottoms Up. Banks already told her he wanted her to keep stripping to get the funds he needed to build *their* empire! She was madly in love with him and would have walked through fire to make sure he got what he needed.

She couldn't wait for them to lay in bed together. Every time she thought about it, it gave her chills. She motioned for him to get the mop and broom. As soon as he stepped in the sally port, she kissed him while nibbling on his bottom lip. In the year and a half, they had minimal contact. Since she planned on quitting anyway, she threw caution to the wind.

Banks licked his lips after tasting her cherry red lip gloss. "I can't wait to fuck you down tonight!"

"Boy...You better. You've been having me fiending. All that phone sex, plus me having to watch you jack that big ole dick off in your cell." After he squeezed her ass and cuffed her pussy, he went back into the tank. Heading straight to the cell where Serve was waiting on him.

"Say young P, I've given you everything you need to succeed. I really feel as though you were born with a pair of gators on. You just had to realize it. Now, the games a bitch, but all bitches can be pimped. Respect the game, play by the rules and I guarantee you, you'll be king!"

Banks soaked up every word and dissected every morsel of game Serve blessed him with. Serve was scheduled to go to trial on his murder case in 2 months. Bank's heart hurt for his friend. Serve felt like he had a little action, but with his age, any sentence was a life sentence.

The last offer was 40 years. He felt like he had no choice but to take it to trial. Banks really looked at Serve like a father and wished he could do something to help him out. It was *him* that pushed Banks to go after Tracy. It was *him* that taught Banks the ins and outs about hustling in jail?

"Say Unc, you got my word. I'ma play the game how it go. I respect you too much to dirty your name out here as a nigga that came up under your pimping. Plus, I'll pay you what you deserve for this top shelf game you've bestowed upon me," Banks confessed to Serve.

"Banks...ATW!" Tracy practically screamed over the intercom. She couldn't contain herself. Even doing a little jig in the picket.

Serve gave Banks a great big bear hug. "I know you'll do right P...When the time comes, I'll be here."

Banks left all his commissary and appliances to Serve. Orin had already bonded out, so Serve was the only person he felt obligated to. He also made sure Tracy deposited $3,000 on his books, because Banks knew all of Serve's hoes had left him while he was fighting the case. He told Banks. "Never be mad at a hoe for choosing up while you're in jail. After all, you're not out there to perform your duties, so why should you be paid."

As Banks was leaving, a few officers he had gotten cool with congratulated him. Some females even went as far as to give him their contact info. Sex was the last thing on his mind though. He still took their info. Every bitch deserved an interview. Only requirements were 2 legs to walk to the money and at least 1 hand to hand it over.

When he stepped outside for the first time in over a year and a half, he was amazed at how much the world had changed in such a short amount of time. He thought about everything he lost while he was gone. If it wasn't for Tracy, he would have nowhere else to go. He cashed his Inmate Trust Fund check and caught an Uber to *their* apartment.

As he exited Normandy, he began to think of Chrissy and wondered where the hell she had burned off too. He quickly shook his thought, as he turned into the apartments.

The Pines was a cool little duck off spot. It wasn't "hood" like Hunterwood or Coolwood, but it was hood enough for a street nigga to feel comfortable.

He told the driver what apartment he was looking for and got dropped off right at the front door. He searched for the spare key Tracy had left for him. Once he found it, he opened the door and wasn't surprised. Everything was neat and tidy. He remembered her saying something about buying him some clothes, so he went straight to the closet to see what type of drip she bought him.

He picked out a red Polo shirt, black Polo shorts and some red and black Retro 11's. He took a long hot "free world" shower. Once he dried off, he inspected his new cologne collection. He picked up a bottle of Kenneth Cole Black and applied just the right amount. He looked at his Michael Kors watch. He had 4 hours before Tracy got off work. He decided to take a walk through the apartment complex.

After about 5 minutes of walking, he came across a little Blood homie, posted up against a Buick LeSabre. "What it is? What that B like," the youngster questioned.

"Bloody days, Bloody ways," Banks responded while locking up the B's with the youngster.

"Say Blood...Where they got that Loud at around here?"

"Shit...Blood, you looking at it. What you need?"

Banks had about $200 on him, with a check for $1,580. "Just shoot me an 8. How much?"

"Since you a homie, I'll give you the 8 for $35!"

"That's a bet!"

"Do you need some rillos too?" The youngster asked while pulling out 2 Swisha Sweet cigarillos.

"You know what...Yeah, fuck with me. That'll save me a trip to the store." After he twisted one up, he blew it with the youngster.

"So, what they call you," the youngster asked.

"Bankroll."

The youngster's eyes lit up at the mention of Banks street name.

"Bankroll? From Hunterwood? Man, they said you had gotten the death penalty," he informed Banks.

Banks laughed. "Well, as you can see...I'm here in the flesh...What they call you," he added, trying to get the focus off him.

"D-Will. My big homie is Titan from Rosewood." Banks knew Titan. Titan was a solid nigga. He hustled hard and had at least 3 bodies Banks knew about. So, if the apple didn't fall far from the tree, he knew D-Will should have been at least half as solid. After politicking for a few more minutes, Banks locked up with him. Told him he would *"Bee"* him later and kept breezing through the complex. As he bent a corner, he heard some loud commotion.

Some heavy-set dude had a brown skin chick hemmed up against a car.

WHAP!

He slapped her so hard, Banks could hear her skin spit from 40 yards away. "Bitch...You want to play me like a sucka? I knew you was fucking the nigga Keith," dude yelled out.

"Black! Pleeassee stop hitting me! I didn't fuck anybody. Man, you tripping," the female cried out while holding her face. A part of Banks wanted to help, but this shit was none of his business. Now, *if* she was his hoe, and socking it to his pockets, then he would stand in front of death himself, to prevent him from laying a finger on her head. As of right now, she wasn't. So, he just sat back and watched the show as Black continued to pummel the girl.

She couldn't take any more abuse. Instead of trying to fight back, she hit the ground and balled up in the fetal position. That didn't deter Black. He decided to put his size 12 Adidas into her ribs. He even went as far as to kick her in her ass.

"Agghh Black...Please stop. I swear I didn't do shit. Why you doing me like this?" After a while, Black must have realized that someone could have called the police. After all, she was screaming bloody murder. He hawked a loogy, spit on her, kicked her one more time for good measure, then hopped in his 96' Chevy Impala SS and got the hell out of dodge.

Banks first mind was to keep going. He was fresh out and didn't need to be tied up in no bullshit.

Seeing her in distress, he decided to go ahead and check on her. Just to make sure she was alright.

"Say lil' momma, you aight over here," Banks asked sincerely.

She looked up. Tears and snot covered her face. "Leave me alone man. This ain't none of your bidness." Banks had to admit. Even though she was worse for wear, she was still an extremely beautiful woman. He didn't want to just leave her, but what else could he do? She just didn't want to be bothered. He pulled out his sack, and twisted up another blunt, right there on the spot.

As soon as the blunt was lit, he hit it twice. The female seemed to calm down a bit, after she smelled the sweet scent of the Loud burning. She raised her head up. Banks held out the cigarillo. "You wanna hit this?" She hesitated. He shrugged his shoulders, then hit it again. "Okay, your loss."

She began to pick herself off the ground. Once she stood all the way up, he got a much better look at her. Shorty was bad! About 5'4", 145 lbs. She was all hips and ass. Her titties had to be small B's and her face. So gorgeous! He offered her the blunt once again. This time, she accepted it. She hit it twice and attempted to give it back. "Naw, go ahead and keep hitting it. I had a head start after all."

After he felt she was all the way relaxed, he started his inquiry. "What's your name?"

"Raven... But everybody calls me Ms. Pretty."

"I see why." He watched as she blushed from his last remark. After about 15 minutes of conversation, she offered Banks something to drink. He accepted and followed her to her apartment.

From their initial conversation, he knew she stayed with her dope fiend momma, who was never at home.

"Probably out chasing her next high." As she put it. He had also learned, Black was her boyfriend. He was tripping because, he heard from his patna Karl, that she had supposedly fucked another one of their homeboys named Keith. Basically, a bunch of he said, she said bullshit.

Banks didn't ask if she fucked Keith and honesty he didn't care if she did. She brought him a soda then said, "I'll be right back". Then, she disappeared into the bedroom.

He heard the shower running, grabbed the remote and started flipping through the channels. He watched a little bit of Love and Hip Hop, remembering the flick he downloaded of Mimi getting fucked in the shower.

A sudden presence could be felt standing over him. When he looked up, Pretty was standing there in some pink and blue boy shorts and a Hello Kitty tank top. Her ass was so fat, the back of the boy shorts damn near looked like a pair of thongs. His dick began to stiffen.

She sat down next to him and began to watch TV. Banks pulled out the last cigarillo, placed the rest of the loud into it, and twisted up. They smoked and laughed at reruns of Martin.

Banks looked at his watch and saw it was time to go. Tracy would be home soon, and he needed to be at the spot to welcome her back. As he stood up, Pretty's hand shot to his lap, caressing his dick through his Polo shorts. She had that look in her eyes that said she would not be denied. Even though his dick wanted too, Banks forced himself to remove her hand. *"Never trick your dick off. Only the ones that pay it, you lay with."* He heard Serve's voice echoing loudly in his head. "Naw, I'm good right now, baby girl. Maybe next time."

He gave her a hug and headed to the door. Pretty stood there disappointed, but at the same time astonished with admiration. Niggas didn't turn her down. At all! Shit, Keith paid her just to eat her ass. Then, he paid her some more. Just to eat some pussy until she creamed all over his tongue.

She knew Banks wanted to fuck. His dick told her so. So, why not? As she closed the door behind him, she vowed to herself. She would find out why before it was said and done. She was going to get some of that dick he was cuffing.

"I'm telling you Blood. That nigga's got some serious bread. He's supposed to have like $2-$3 mill put up," Marlo aka Khamp said. He'd been trying to convince NOB for the last 20 minutes on why they should press play on their next target. NOB was still unconvinced.

"Son, how you know he got all that shit up in there? Do you got anybody that seen it themselves? I ain't tryna run up in that bitch with them cutters for nothing. Especially, if we gotta step on something, son." NOB was always cautious with every lick he went on. He was always someone who crossed the T's and dotted the I's. Marlo wasn't giving up though.

"Blood, my bitch used to kick it with one of his hoes. She said each of them pull in no less than $1,500-$2,000 a night. Now, add that to the fact he keeps no less than 5 hoes at a time. Shit, do the math. The pussy ass niggas been at it for years? At the very least, we'll hit him for no less than a half a mill ticket. Even that would be worth it."

NOB began to warm up to the idea. There was only one problem. "The nigga ain't out and about like that. So how we supposed to pinpoint where he keep the bulk of his stash at," NOB asked. Neither one of them had the answer. After sitting in silence for about 15 minutes, a light bulb went off in NOB's head. He had an idea.

Damn this shit stinks!, Dorian thought as Paccy fired up a Sherm stick. Even though she would indulge every now and then, Sherm was definitely her least favorite drug of all. The only plus side? When Paccy got full of it, he would go ape shit on her pussy. He would fuck her without mercy. Until she tapped out or blacked out. Either way, she would not be spared. So, if she couldn't handle no more dick, she would get her mouth fucked like it was her pussy part 2 until he came.

He usually only smoked when he had something to celebrate. What were they celebrating? They hadn't hit a lick in almost a month. The last one they hit *was* Troy. Now, she was addicted to the rush. She needed one to sedate her hunger. Every time she approached Paccy about another lick, his response would always be the same. "Now right now? The streets are too hot!"

They had a *little* bread put up. After they gapped everything down with J-Bang, they had a little over 100k. *I know he ain't satisfied with that!,* she thought. She excused herself and went outside to get some fresh air. She pulled out her phone and dialed her best friend's number.

"Heyy girl," Chrissy yelled into the phone? It sounded like she was in a club. Dorian looked at the time? It was 10:30 pm. *What club is popping this early?* She knew Chrissy no longer worked at Club Heat, but she had no clue that her friend was full-fledged ho'ing.

"Bitch, where you at," Dorian asked.

"I'm in the A, getting to that money babbbyyy!," Chrissy screamed excitedly.

"Atlanta? Did you say Atlanta?"

"Yeah bitch...Atlanta. You should come out here? It's turnt the fuck up," Chrissy encouraged.

That's why the clubs popping right now. They're time zones ahead of us. "Maybe one of these days I will," she said, not really believing it. Dorian always wanted to travel, but never seemed to have the means. Now that she had the money, she didn't really have the urge to travel.

"Well...I'll only be here a couple more days, then I'm headed to Miami," Chrissy informed her.

"Damn! What, you globetrotting now," Dorian asked with a little more jealousy in her tone than she would've liked.

"Naw, I'm just on my grind boo... You can sleep when you die!"

"I know that's right," Dorian said as she thought about Paccy and how he'd been slacking as of late. "Well, let me let you get back to your bag...And don't be a stranger!"

"Aight girl. Well, I love you."

"I love you too," Dorian said as she hung up. Now, she was beginning to wonder what it would be like to travel. Maybe her and Paccy could take their show on the road. Her phone rang.

"Hello," she answered.

"Wassup Crystal...What's been up," the male voice asked. Dorian had to look at the screen again. She noticed the name and number but couldn't put a face to it. The contact said

Fish. She flipped through her mental rolodex. *Oh shit..Fish!,* she finally realized.

Fish was a big-time hustler out of 5th Ward. He was getting major weight and supplying most of the Northside. She was about to start finessing him but remembered *Damn...Too bad Paccy doesn't want to hit any licks right now.*

Then she was like, Fuck that! There is no way she's throwing this *Fish* back in the water. Why not work on the fool until Paccy was ready to move.

"Heyyy Fish. What took you so long to call me? I gave you my number like 3 weeks ago," she said with a little bit of an attitude.

"Yeah, I know. I have just been hella busy lately, but I'm tryna catch up with you now. What you got planned?"

"Well, I'm busy tonight, but we can link up tomorrow if you're not doing anything," she stated.

"That's a bet then, sexy," Fish told her as they wrapped their conversation up. Now, all she had to do was figure out a way to duck and dodge Paccy.

The next day, Dorian woke up with a swollen cat. Courtesy of the royal fucking Paccy gave her the night before. She lost count of how many times she nutted, but she knew it was at least 6-7 times. She could taste the fuck on her breath. *What do you expect, when you swallow a gallon of cum?*

She rolled over and noticed Paccy was gone. She felt like he must have been in the living room. Somehow, she found the strength to get out of bed, and hopped in the shower.

As the hot water sprayed away the remnants of sweat, sex and sleep, she couldn't help but to think about Fish. She still didn't know how she would shake Paccy for the night, but she was determined to figure it out. She *had* to meet up with Fish. No matter what!

After she dried herself off, she threw on some black tights and a blue wife beater. Since she was around the house, it really didn't matter what she wore. She knew Paccy wasn't about to boil water, much less cook. She hit the kitchen to whip them up something to eat.

Soon as she stepped into the living room, she noticed Paccy at the coffee table sniffing some type of substance. She couldn't tell if it was coke until she got a little closer and saw it had a brownish hue to it. *Is he fucking with that boy now?*

Paccy heard her footsteps and slowly picked his head up. Eyes glazed and half closed. He gave her an early morning greeting. "Heyyy baabbbee!" She walked up and investigated further.

She looked at the powdered substance. Then at Paccy and asked, "Soooo. You fucking with that boy now?" Paccy looked down at the dope as if seeing it for the first time. He looked up at her and said, "What?...You want some?"

"Want some? Wants some! Nigga, is you crazy? I'm not fucking with that shit. What I'm trynna figure out, is when did you start?" Dorian yelled.

She knew exactly when it started. After he had to bury his best friend behind his supposed betrayal. Then, he lost his lil' homie, plus all his money shortly after.

Dorian felt fucked up. She was the one responsible for Dread getting killed. But shit, the bastard had it coming. He was blackmailing her for pussy and head aka *rape motherfucker!* She looked at Paccy, shook her head and walked off. Leaving him to continue doing what he was doing.

She couldn't help but to notice how Paccy was falling off, right before her very eyes. She loved him, but she didn't know how to fix the situation.

Shaking Paccy turned out to be easier than she expected. After playing with his nose all day, he took himself out of the game and passed out on the couch. He'd been going hard for the last 3 or 4 days straight. His body decided it couldn't take anymore. Dorian called Fish, set their date up, while Paccy sat on the couch drooling over himself.

After hopping back into the shower, she went to her closet and pulled out an aqua blue, skintight mini dress. No bra and of course, no panties. She threw on some Jimmy Choo's and grabbed a Gucci clutch. Taking one more look at Paccy, she shook her head and walked out the door.

She and Fish decided to meet at Boudreaux's on 610 South. They were known for their alligator dish. That's exactly what Fish ordered. After a few drinks, their conversation began to flow freely

"Sooo...Mr. Fish, tell me, why is it you don't have a woman," Dorian opened up.

"Well, honestly...I haven't found one I felt comfortable around. Most women know I have a lil' bread, so that's the first thing that comes out their mouths. "Can I have this?" Or "Can I borrow that?" I need a woman that can get it on her own, and if we come up together, then we could definitely cause some damage."

Dorian smiled, because that's exactly the facade she paints to entrap her victims. Once a man feels like you're not after his money, then he won't have any problems spending it on you OR, letting you know where it's kept.

"I can definitely feel that," she replied. Waiting on him to ask the same question.

"So, why don't you have a man?" *So predictable.*

"Well, I'm the type of woman that scares most men. Since I have my own shit, I don't need a man for anything, except when I need my cat scratched. Plus, where I'm from in North Carolina, the men ain't 'bout shit no way. I'm hoping that since I'm in Texas, I'll get a chance to see what a real man out here's like."

Dorian always made sure she had an alternative persona whenever she approached potential licks. This includes name, D.O.B., place of birth, even what high school she attended. Paccy taught her to know her origins. Know the streets in the areas she claimed to be from. So, she googled hot spots in North Carolina. Streets as well as historical events and landmarks. Just in case her victim had ever visited the area.

Her and Fish definitely hit it off. After a few more rounds, he decided to make his move. He got up to use the restroom, and when he came back, he slid in the booth next to her.

Dorian welcomed the advance. When he was close enough, he slipped his hand between her thighs. He felt her wetness immediately! She let him dip his fingers in her twat before she closed her legs shut! "Not today," she whispered. She slowly removed his hand and placed those same fingers in her mouth. Slowly sucking the juices off. "Now, clean up after yourself," she told him. Without hesitation, he stuck the digits in his mouth, leaving them clean as a whistle.

Fish smacked his lips and said, "Damn! Your pussy tastes better than anything they had on the menu." Dorian smiled, got up, then scooted out the booth. Making sure her fat ass booty rubbed against the front of his pants. Fish's dick was so hard, he had to wait until his erection went down before he could follow her to the car.

As they both stood in the parking lot, Dorian allowed Fish to feel her up. Making sure he touched every part of her body; except the parts he craved the most.

After saying their goodbyes, Fish hopped inside his root beer Range. He caught a quick peek at Dorian getting inside of her Beamer. As she swung her legs into the car, he got a clear view of her freshly shaved, plump pussy lips. He squeezed his dick as it ached. He made a promise to himself. When he got the chance to tap that, he was going to fuck her into submission. Dorian stayed on his mind all night. Just the way she wanted it.

The last night in the A and so far the girls made $158,626 total. By far, the most any 2 girls in Saints stable had made in a 3-week period. A lot of that had to do with Sache. When he wasn't giving her money outright, he was taking her and

Peaches to clubs all over the city. Just so niggas could "rain" on them. What he really was doing, was making sure he was the only dick she was getting at the end of the night. *He thinks he's slick.* She wasn't tripping though. He actually had some good dick, and he was worth his weight in gold. Why not let him believe they had a steady thing going?

It was almost 4 in the morning. Chrissy and Peaches were at a hotel party. Some local rappers from the A, decided to come together and rent out 3 Presidential suites. Since they were leaving to go to Miami the next day, the girls figured they could use their 5 finger discounts to come up on a little extra bread.

It would work out well, because there were a lot of out-of-town cats that would never see, much less recognize them amongst all the other girls that were entertaining.

Chrissy had developed a decent pickpocket game, but Peaches was masterful. She would work her pussy lips around a wallet or knot while she gave the customer a lap dance. Every so often, pushing the prize further and further up their pockets until finally, it falls to the floor. Then, she would discreetly pick it up while signaling another dancer to come relieve her. That way she could stash away the loot.

Of course, she had to break the accomplice dancer off. Because if shit were to hit the fan, her name would be thrown in the hat also.

Chrissy was giving a sensual lap dance to one of Atlanta's local rappers named Dice Dollars. She slyly watched Peaches servicing one of the out-of-town cats. Chrissy watched in awe as Peaches "worked clean". As soon as the other stripper had approached to get a lap dance in, Chrissy knew Peaches had struck.

She couldn't do anything but smile. She had to tilt her hat. The hoe Peaches got it in by any means necessary. She had wondered why Saint had paired them together. Now, she was glad that he did. She was soaking up everything she could from Peaches. She learned so much in the last 3 weeks. Now, she was eager to learn more.

Sache was also at the party, but it was obvious his mind was preoccupied with something else. Earlier that evening, he'd received a disturbing call. Ever since then, he'd been in a sour mood.

Chrissy tried to cheer him up with a private show. He just shook her off. *Fuck it!* She continued to work the crowd and was lucky when one of her tricks was so drunk that when he tried to put his wallet back into his pocket, it slipped and fell on the floor. *He deserved to get got,* Chrissy thought to herself as she signaled for a relief stripper. When one arrived, she discreetly picked up the wallet and headed to go stash it.

The night was going well, until one of the less experienced thieves got her hand caught in the cookie jar. A dancer by the name of Cookie, tried to make off with an out of towner named Chubbs's knot. He grabbed her wrist and proceeded to viciously back hand her.

SMACK! SMACK! SMACK!

She fell backwards and landed on one of the rappers from the A, causing him to spill his cup of liquor all over his designer apparel. Then, all hell broke loose!

Another Atlanta rapper took his bottle of Rosé and smacked Chubbs across the face with it. A soft crack was heard as the bottle shattered Chubbs's nose but didn't break. Blood gushed forth and saturated his shirt. He struggled to maintain his balance.

Then suddenly, a few Atlanta rappers pulled out blades and started sticking anyone who was from out of town. They didn't care if they had something to do with it or not. Chaos officially erupted.

Blood was everywhere. Chrissy set out to find Peaches. Finally, she found her in the bathroom handing her relief stripper, Shade, a stack of money for her part. "Bitch we gotta go! Them niggas out there tripping. They cutting each other up!" Chrissy screamed in panic.

"What!" Peaches was shocked. She'd been oblivious to what had been going on a few feet away from the bathroom door. As they came out, they noticed damn near everybody was gone. You had a few dudes lying around. *Literally!*

"I think them niggas dead Peaches," Chrissy whispered as if they would rise from the dead if they overhead. Peaches' eyes started darting back and forth, appraising the situation.

"Chrissy, find our shit so we can get the hell out of here!" Shade was already heading out the door. As Chrissy tried to locate their stuff, Peaches was going in pockets as they laid lifeless on the blood soaked carpet. *This bitch is ruthless!,* Chrissy thought as she finally found their suitcases. As they made their way out of the hotel, they heard sirens in the distance.

They hurriedly called Saint and informed him about the crisis. "Don't head back to y'all's room. Even though y'all used fake ID's. I still don't want the chance of someone from the party seeing y'all. They might consider y'all loose ends and try to tie y'all up.

Peaches continued to listen as they climbed into their rental car. She placed him on speaker so she wouldn't have to repeat himself to Chrissy. "Drive to the nearest town. Get a room at a hole in the wall motel," Saint directed as they hit a backstreet, headed to the freeway. "What y'all bring in?"

Chrissy was the first to answer. "Well Daddy, I only brought in $2,800 because all that extra shit had popped off.

"That's understandable...That's why I don't like servicing parties with young black men. That's almost always the situation," Saint told them. "What about you Peaches? What your trap look like?" Chrissy expected Peaches to tell him she brought in at least $4-$5,000. Plus, what she found in jewelry.

Instead, she responded, "Daddy, it was hella slow. I only brought in $1,800, but I'm a see 'bout turning a trick before we leave for Miami in the morning. Chrissy looked at

Peaches out the corner of her eye. *What the fuck?*" she asked herself.

Chrissy couldn't understand why she didn't tell Saint about what she found in them niggas pockets. Chrissy knew for a fact, Peaches made 3x that amount. She thought Peaches was the most loyal hoe she'd ever met. Now, she had to rethink that. Saint told them to call him as soon as they checked into a new room. Then, he disconnected the call.

They rode in silence for a few miles. Each one, deep in her own thoughts. Chrissy suddenly realized she didn't know what happened to Sache. She picked up her phone and tried to dial his number.

'BUMP!BUMP!'

The rental car leaped off its axle as it ran over something in the road. Peaches had been caught off guard. She nearly lost control of the wheel as the car fishtailed before coming to a complete stop in the middle of a dark and deserted service road.

At 4 something in the morning, both women were leery about getting out and investigating what caused the accident. After a moment of silent stares, Chrissy decided to get out and look. With her knees and hands shaking harder than a Parkinson patient, she took baby steps towards what appeared to be a dead animal. She prayed it was dead. If it wasn't, she'd surely shit on herself.

As she crept closer, she was able to distinguish the features and her heart sank to her stomach. It wasn't an animal. It was... A body! Half of the head was missing. The street was drenched in blood. The person's arm was twisted back and broken at an abnormal angle. A bone was poking through the flesh where the elbow should have been.

Chrissy wretched and almost threw up. She forced her feet to move a little closer. Her heart thundered in her chest cavity. Her body trembled. Cold sweat flowed down her prickly skin. She got within 2 feet of the body and screamed. *Cookie!*

The same one who got caught with her hand in Chubb's pocket. The one that set off the chain of events. She looked at the body closely and realized there were gunshot wounds in both palms.

"Damn...That's some fucked up shit!," she cursed herself.

"Chrissy!...What the hell is that," Peaches yelled from the safety of her driver's seat. Chrissy turned to tell her, but her voice got caught in her throat when she saw a pair of headlights approaching about 400 yards away. Instantly, her street senses kicked in. She took off running back towards her car.

"Bitch. Go! Go! Go!" She yelled. Fortunately Peaches wisely didn't ask why, she just put the pedal to the metal. Chrissy crossed her fingers and hoped like hell it wasn't a cop car they were approaching. *Whoooo!* It wasn't!

Instead, they passed up an SUV as they made their way out of that God forsaken town. Chrissy checked the rearview mirror and saw the SUV come to an abrupt stop. "Bitch! We need to get the fuck up outta here. NOW!" She growled. Peaches mashed the gas even more. Taking them to the next town on the way to their next destination.

Chapter 15

As Banks collapsed on the king size mattress, sweat dripping from his pores, he had to admit. Tracy might have the best pussy he ever had. Soon as she'd gotten off of work, they went at it hot and heavy. After they got that first nut out the way, they both got in the shower, washing each other's bodies off, before they spent the rest of the night in bed.

He licked, sucked, kissed and nibbled, until he had her seeing stars. After 4 continuous orgasms, Tracy threw in the towel. Promising to get back at him when she caught her breath.

"Damn babe...I see you got a lot of pent-up stress. You gone fuck around and have me walking round this bitch bowlegged," Tracy laughed as she relit the blunt that was in the ashtray. After she hit it twice, she passed it to Banks.

"You know I gotta do you right," he said while massaging the inside of her thighs. "You put everything on the line to help a nigga get free. You believed in me as a man, and as the Boss that I am." He lifted her chin so they could see eye to eye. "I promise baby, I got you. I'll never turn my back on you. As long as you're by my side, we'll never be defeated." Two lone tears rolled down Tracy's cheek. Banks used his thumb to wipe them away.

Tracy's heart pounded in her chest. She was so scared. Scared because Banks had her heart completely. He had the power to destroy her very essence if he chose too. She would do anything for him. Her loyalty was absolute. Banks felt it was time for him to reveal his plans for the future.

"Look baby, you've been rocking with a nigga the harder way. Like I said, you're the sole reason I'm out right now. I don't wanna fuck with that dope no more. It's much too risky these days. Especially if I have to find a new plug. Sooo...I want to try my hand at Pimping." Tracy flinched then recoiled, as if she tasted something bitter. He could see the hurt and confusion in her eyes.

"What did you just say nigga? You mean to tell me, I ride it out with you expecting a ring on my finger and you tell me you 'bout to surround yourself with hoes. That you want me to be one of many." He tried to grab her hands, but she slapped his hand away and stormed into the bathroom.

She slammed the door shut, sat on the toilet and cried her eyes out. *I should've known he was gone get on some pimp shit. He stayed up under Serve's motherfucking ass for too long!,* she thought as she cried.

'Knock. Knock. Knock.' Banks knocked, then twisted the knob. The door was locked. "Tracy, listen baby, nothing has changed and nothing will change. You're my Alpha and you'll be my Omega. I just don't want to put myself in a position where I'll be taken away from you. No matter how many hoes I get, no one will come before you. It's not like I plan on doing this until I die. Just ride it out with me. I promise, it'll be worth it. I don't want to do this without you, but I *will* do it without you."

Tracy's heart dropped. There it was. If she wanted to be with him, then she had to get with the program! She used to laugh at all those silly hoes who grinded all night in the club, just to give all their money to a nigga who call himself a Pimp. She laughed at the irony. Now *she* was considering being up under a nigga pimping.

But was it the same? Her and Banks were more than just business partners. More than just pimp and hoe. She loved him with all her heart, and couldn't see herself being with anybody else. Right then, she knew what her decision would be. She would be his hoe. Shit...Truth be told, she already was.

She stood up and unlocked the door. She opened it. Banks was sitting on the floor with his back against the door. He saw her, turned and quickly got on his feet. She looked him in the eyes. Tears streaming from hers.

"Brandon...I love you with all my heart. More than I've loved anyone else. Because of that love, I'll forever be loyal to you. I wanna make you happy. If that's what I have to do to ensure that, so be it. But...I swear, if you fuck over me, you will regret it!"

Her words sent chills down his spine. Something told him she was serious as a heart attack. He gave her a great big hug, holding her tightly. He listened as she cried on his shoulder. "Baby, I'll never fuck over you. You're my foundation. Without you, I will surely crumble," Banks assured her as he grabbed her hand and led her back into bed.

After licking her tears away, Banks licked and sucked on her pussy until she screamed and creamed all over his lips. As they both laid in bed, Banks explained to her about the rules of the game, and what's expected from her. Once he quizzed her and felt secure that she retained all of the information, he called it a night. Tomorrow would be his first official day as a Pimp, and he couldn't wait to get started.

He just wonders if Tracy was going to be able to handle the transition, from square to game. Only time would tell. He sure hoped so. He really cared for her, and he would hate to hand her walking papers after everything she'd done for him. Make no mistake, he would if he had too.

As Tracy stood in the mirror with nothing but a black thong, preparing her makeup, Banks couldn't help but to feel his dick stir. She was thick as hell and that pussy was oh so good. He decided to grab a quickie.

He pulled out his semi erect dick and slid it between her ass cheeks. A soft moan escaped her lips. She reached back, grabbed his piece and stroked him until he became full mast. With her other hand, she pulled her thong to the side, bent over the bathroom counter and guided that missile home.

"Ahh shit... Damn, Daddy. I love this big ole dick," she growled as Banks began to stroke her deep and hard. Honey dripped from her coochie as he dug her out. Her ass cheeks clapping as he tore into her. "Ooohh. Fuck me, Daddy. Make this pussy cum all over that big ass dick." *"Keep your dick out of them because their emotions will always get the better of them. Eventually, she'll be worried 'bout where you put your dick instead of where to get your money."* Banks heard Serve's voice in his head, as he pounded into Tracy's sopping wet cunt.

He pushed the thought out his mind as he announced, "Fuck!...Bitch, I'm 'bout to cum!" Tracy slid off, allowing his dick to fall out. She turned around and dropped to her knees. Banks gave his meat 6 pumps before his hot nut splashed on Tracy's waiting tongue

"Ummm," she hummed and smacked her lips as she licked the dick clean. She kissed the tip, then told him, "I got to get ready to go get this money, Daddy.. You gone have a bitch too tired to work!

He slapped her on her soft ass and said, "Yeah right! My bitches can hoe in their sleep 8 days out the week." He left her to get dressed and decided to step outside and smoke him a cigarette. He also wanted to hit D-Will up and see if he had any more Loud on deck. As he sat on the balcony, he noticed a burnt orange Roadmaster creeping down the street. He knew burnt orange was a color they sprayed their cars with on the East. Especially the Insane Guerilla Family.

He watched the car suspiciously. He wished he had a pole on him. He'd heard a bunch of rumors that Paccy was the one that hit him for his stash. Niggas were coming to the county talking about how Paccy had turnt all the way, soon as he went to jail.

He still felt like Chrissy had something to do with it. Especially once he found out her best friend was fucking with Paccy now. In jail you get news quicker than CNN, Fox or ABC13. It hurt him to think Chrissy would do some dirty shit like that. But then again, she stopped accepting his calls. And, she stopped coming to see him. She called herself writing a few letters, but Banks wasn't trying to hear that shit. He didn't bother to read them. So as soon as they hit his hands, he threw them in the trash.

He watched the Roadmaster come to a complete stop in front of Raven's crib. Minutes later, she came out in some low-cut Apple Bottom jeans with a spaghetti strap shirt. *Damn shorty is thick as fuck!*, he told himself as he watched her ass jiggle from 20 feet away.

As if sensing him staring, right before she hopped in the car, she locked eyes with him and smiled. Banks told himself then, before it was said and done, she would be in his stable. First, he had to find out who that nigga was in the orange Roadmaster.

'Slam!' Dorian slammed the door to the condo. She angrily walked towards the car. Once again Paccy was on some bullshit. Talking 'bout the streets was too hot. Lately, all he'd been doing is getting high. For the last few months, Dorian has been putting in leg work on Fish. Now was the time to get at him.

She made him wait a month to get the goods. When he finally got a taste of it, she unleashed the freak on him and now he was hooked like his namesake. He even introduced her to his parents as his girlfriend. Taking her to the spot where he laid his head.

After spiking his drink with handlebars, she took time to locate the safe. She took pictures of every room. By the moves he was making, she estimated Fish had at least a half a ticket put up. When she told Paccy she had another lick that was ripe for the picking, he dismissed her with the wave of a hand. "Let shit die down," he said. Dorian looked at him like he was retarded. *What the fuck?*

"It's been over 3 months since that shit with Troy," she told him. "The heat been done died down. Shit, it's getting chilly outside," she spat sarcastically.

Paccy snapped his neck in her direction. "What did I say? Bitch, I run the show. When you grow a set of balls, then you can tell me what to do?"

She knew she shouldn't have, but she couldn't resist. "Well, it seems like you've lost your set. When I find them, I'll let you know."

Like a viper, he shot out of his seat, slapped her so hard, she saw stars dance behind her eyelids. "Bitch! You wanna stand there and disrespect me," Paccy roared, while pulling his belt loose. Before she knew it, he was whipping her viciously. "What you think, I'm pussy or something? That's what you trynna say," he yelled while beating her like a stepchild who stole his wallet.

Dorian screamed. "Stop! Please Paccy. Stop hitting me!" But he was unrelenting. After what seemed like minutes, but was mere seconds, he stopped hitting her. Paccy kicked her in the ribs before he walked off, slamming the door behind him.

About a month ago, Paccy had started to put his hands on her. It seemed like the beatings were getting worse each time. Her skin burned, her ribs ached, but she forced herself to get back up. She put up with the beatings, because she felt guilty. She knew that him killing Dread was weighing heavy on his conscience, and that's why he was slowly losing it.

"Fuck it. If he don't wanna hit the lick, I'll hit it myself," she said aloud as she sat in the car. She put it in drive, grabbed her phone and dialed.

"Ayyee!," an accented voice came through the headset.

"Is this NOB," Dorian asked.

"Yeah...Who dis?"

"This D Money... Chrissy's home girl."

"Oh yeah. Wassup? You got some food for me? Referring to another lick.

"Really, that's why I'm calling. I got something big I'm working on, and I need to sit down and talk to you about it. Are you on the East?"

"Yeah, I'm leaving Pine Trails right now," he answered.

"I'm on Wallisville and Uvalde. Where can we meet?"

"Just come through the spot. Do you know where Uvalde Ranch is," he asked her.

"Yeah, I know where it's at. What apartment do you stay in?"

"115...It's towards the back, by the exit gate."

"Aight bet? Give me like 20 minutes," she said before hanging up."

"When she pulled up, she noticed his black Charger, with 2 other vehicles parked next to it. She hoped he was alone. If not, hopefully they will find somewhere private to talk. She dialed his number again.

"Ayyee," he answered.

"I'm outside." Before she could say another word, he hung up. She grabbed her purse and got out the car. She knocked twice on the door. It swung open. Standing there, was a pretty redbone chick, with a stupid fat ass. Dorian didn't mess with girls, but she had to admit. Ole girl had it going on.

Dorian was about to ask her about NOB, but she could tell it was a lot of attitude coming off the chick. She wanted to tell her, " Look, I'm not here for your man." Before she could say anything, ole girl just shuffled by her, clearly not interested in introductions.

As she entered the spot, she was hit with a strong scent of weed and sex. It wasn't a foul smell, but you could tell someone was getting their freak on. That's probably why she was pissed. I would be too, if someone stopped me from getting my back blew out. She looked around the room, and noticed a tall ass, dark skin dude sitting on the couch watching the monitor. He had a Draco with a red bandanna tied around it, sitting on his lap.

She asked him, "Where's NOB at?"

He looked up and pointed to the back bedroom. "He's in there waiting on you."

Thankful for the privacy, she made her way to the bedroom. She heard the shower running. She decided to sit on the bed. Careful not to come in contact with any wet spots. She picked up the remote and turned the TV on. Instantly, a porno began to play. 2 big dick black men were getting serviced by a thick redbone. It had been about a week since she'd gotten some good dick. At that moment, her pussy was dripping, wetting the crotch of her panties. She fantasized about how it would feel to get fucked by 2 niggas.

Just then, NOB walked out of the bedroom with a towel around his waist, and a smile on his face when he caught her watching the porno. *I didn't even hear the shower stop running,* she thought as she watched him walk into the closet to get dressed. She couldn't lie, he was holding down for the slim cats.

He was ripped up. She couldn't keep her eyes off his sizable dick print the towel was unsuccessfully trying to hide. Sensing her watching, he removed the towel. Now she had an unobstructed view. Unless he was tripping, he could have sworn he heard her moan from all the way across the room.

He applied lotion, cologne, then slid on his Perry Ellis boxers. Once he was fully dressed, he stepped out of the closet. Dorian's eyes were glazed over.

"So, wassup? What you wanna talk 'bout," he asked.

"Huh?.." She asked, almost forgetting why she came. NOB had her ready to come on herself. *Bitch focus!*

"Oh yeah...I got a bidness deal for you."

"Okay. What is it?"

"Do you know a nigga from 5th Ward named Fish?" His eyebrow raised at the mention of the name.

"Who don't know Fish?"

"Well, I got him lined up. I need someone to hit it."

"Same as last time," he asked.

"Yeah, but this time, no witnesses," she concluded.

NOB smiled. To him robbery wasn't complete unless you put a body on it. Now she was taking his language. Only thing left was to figure out the particulars. Which they did.

As Fish turned out of the Tinseltown parking lot, Crystal's phone rang.

"Girrrl," she sang. Even though Fish couldn't hear the other end of her conversation, he figured she must've been on the phone with one of her homegirls. "Yeah, we just seen that new Tyler Perry movie girl. What? That motherfucka was funny as fuck. What you mean who is we? *We* is me and my man. No, he don't wanna talk to you. I don't know, hold on." Dorian turned to Fish and asked.

"Are we headed to the house right now?"

"Baby...It's up to you," he told her.

"Well...In that case, yeah. We heading home bitch," Dorian said before hanging up. He smiled at that. He was really starting to feel Crystal. Not only was she fine as hell, but she could fuck like a porn star. What man doesn't love a freak?

As if reading his mind, Crystal leaned over and gave his dick a nice squeeze. "Can I have a taste of that milk chocolate?" She didn't even wait for an answer. She unzipped his fly, not even bothering to unbuckle his jeans. She reached in, found his dick and pulled it out of the hole in his boxers. She dropped her head into his lap. As she sucked and slurped, Fish could barely pay attention to the road, much less the Charger that was following 3 cars behind.

Usually Crystal would make him cum in less than 5 minutes. This time though, she was taking her sweet time. Slowly sucking on the head, as she massaged the shaft. By the time they got to the crib, he was ready to explode and couldn't wait until they got inside.

They raced through the door. As soon as they crossed the threshold, Crystal dropped to her knees to finish what she had started. After Fish came in her mouth, she swallowed everything, but continued to lick gently until. Within no time, Fish was up and ready again.

She pulled him into the bedroom. After countless orgasms, he finally passed out. Dorian picked up the phone and texted the signal. She unlocked the front door and found a hiding spot in the bathroom.

When she heard the unmistakable sound of metal against flesh, she knew it had begun. She cracked the door open and peeked into the bedroom. For some reason, this part always got her pussy wetter than actual sex.

WHAP!

NOB smacked Fish again with the heavy .45. Blood spewed from his mouth along with a tooth.

"Please man...Don't kill me," Fish begged with his hands up in front of him.

"Where's the safe at, bitch nigga," NOB growled as he smacked him again with the gun.

WHAP!

Based on the pictures Dorian had taken, the safe was supposed to have been in the master bedroom. Apparently, Fish had moved it.

"It's in the wall behind the dresser man...Look, just take it! I don't wanna die," Fish pleaded. NOB grabbed him by the back of his neck, while Marlo pushed the dresser out the way.

Once they had located it, NOB "convinced" Fish to give them the combination. Finally, the safe was opened. No one expected to see what they saw. Inside, was no more than $20,000...Total! *BOCKA!*

NOB blew the back of Fish's head off. Blood splattered on his shirt and shoes, but he wasn't tripping. Everything would be torched by the end of the night. He kicked him repeatedly. "Bitch. Bitch. Bitch ass nigga," he howled in frustration. He wanted badly to put a bullet in something. Anything!

Dorian was licking her lips. Pussy dripping, on the verge of cumming on herself until she saw the contents of the safe. *$20,000...What the fuck?*

NOB grabbed the measly stacks and threw them in her direction. "I thought you said you were sure this nigga had some major bread. What the fuck is this," he screamed. Veins popping out of his neck. His eyes kept twitching. So was his trigger finger.

Dorian was utterly confused. She *did* her research. The streets said Fish was the man. He supplied a whole bunch of niggas across the city. What she didn't know was, Fish was just the front man for a big-time dealer named Smitty.

Smitty had been in the game since the 80's and had survived by staying out of sight and having niggas playing the front. Fish made a little money, but he liked to gamble. Truth be told, he wasn't that good at it. Even though he looked like a million dollars, he barely had enough to pay the bills.

"Fuucckk," Dorian screamed as fear started to flow through her veins. NOB didn't look to happy. She knew his trigger finger was itching.

"Say bitch, I know you ain't have me and my son come up in here for no punk ass 20 bands," he asked with menace in his voice. He upped the pistol, stalking her down with his finger tapping against the trigger.

Dorian threw her hands up. Trembling with fear. She knew she was dead. She didn't want to die like this. "I asked around and everyone said he was legit. Maybe if you weren't so quick to kill him, he could have taken us to where the real money was at." Dorian hoped that he would see the fault in his move and give her a break."

Wrong move!

That seemed to infuriate him even further. With 2 huge steps, NOB was within arm's reach of Dorian. He grabbed her by the neck, forced her to her knees. "Bitch! Open your motherfucking mouth. I'm blowing your shit loose!" Spit flew from his mouth, landing on her face.

With tears coming down her face, Dorian was forced to her knees. She felt like she was about to piss on herself. "Open up!" He screamed. Dorian couldn't stop shaking. She closed her eyes and opened her mouth wide. She felt the warm barrel of the gun, as it slid against her tongue. She could taste the spent gunpowder on her buds. She said a quick prayer and then...

To be continued...

Lock Down Publications and Ca$h Presents
Assisted Publishing Packages

BASIC PACKAGE	**UPGRADED PACKAGE**
$499	$800
Editing	Typing
Cover Design	Editing
Formatting	Cover Design
	Formatting
ADVANCE PACKAGE	**LDP SUPREME PACKAGE**
$1,200	$1,500
Typing	Typing
Editing	Editing
Cover Design	Cover Design
Formatting	Formatting
Copyright registration	Copyright registration
Proofreading	Proofreading
Upload book to Amazon	Set up Amazon account
	Upload book to Amazon
	Advertise on LDP, Amazon and Facebook Page

***Other services available upon request.
Additional charges may apply

Lock Down Publications
P.O. Box 944
Stockbridge, GA 30281-9998
Phone: 470 303-9761

185

Submission Guideline

Submit the first three chapters of your completed manuscript to ldpsubmissions@gmail.com. In the subject line add **Your Book's Title**. The manuscript must be in a Word Doc file and sent as an attachment. Document should be in Times New Roman, double spaced, and in size 12 font. Also, provide your synopsis and full contact information. If sending multiple submissions, they must each be in a separate email.

Have a story but no way to send it electronically? You can still submit to LDP/Ca$h Presents. Send in the first three chapters, written or typed, of your completed manuscript to:

LDP: Submissions Dept
P.O. Box 944
Stockbridge, GA 30281-9998

DO NOT send original manuscript. Must be a duplicate. Provide your synopsis and a cover letter containing your full contact information.

Thanks for considering LDP and Ca$h Presents.

NEW RELEASES

BLOODLINE OF A SAVAGE 1&2
THESE VICIOUS STREETS 1&2
RELENTLESS GOON
RELENTLESS GOON 2
BY PRINCE A. TAUHID

THE BUTTERFLY MAFIA 1-3
BY FUMIYA PAYNE

A THUG'S STREET PRINCESS 1&2
BY MEESHA

CITY OF SMOKE 2
BY MOLOTTI

STEPPERS 1,2&3
THE REAL BADDIES OF CHI-RAQ
BY KING RIO

THE LANE 1&2
BY KEN-KEN SPENCE

THUG OF SPADES 1&2
LOVE IN THE TRENCHES 2
CORNER BOYS
BY COREY ROBINSON

TIL DEATH 3
BY ARYANNA

THE BIRTH OF A GANGSTER 4
BY DELMONT PLAYER

PRODUCT OF THE STREETS 1&2
BY DEMOND "MONEY" ANDERSON

NO TIME FOR ERROR
BY KEESE

MONEY HUNGRY DEMONS
BY TRANAY ADAMS

Coming Soon from Lock Down Publications/Ca$h Presents

IF YOU CROSS ME ONCE 6
ANGEL V
By Anthony Fields

IMMA DIE BOUT MINE 5
By Aryanna

A THUGS STREET PRINCESS 3
By Meesha

PRODUCT OF THE STREETS 3
By Demond Money Anderson

CORNER BOYS 2
By Corey Robinson

THE MURDER QUEENS 6&7
By Michael Gallon

CITY OF SMOKE 3
By Molotti

CONFESSIONS OF A DOPE BOY
By Nicholas Lock

THA TAKEOVER
By Keith Chandler

BETRAYAL OF A G 2
By Ray Vinci

CRIME BOSS
By Playa Ray

Available Now

RESTRAINING ORDER 1 & 2
By **CA$H & Coffee**

LOVE KNOWS NO BOUNDARIES 1-3
By **Coffee**

RAISED AS A GOON I, II, III & IV
BRED BY THE SLUMS I, II, III
BLAST FOR ME I & II
ROTTEN TO THE CORE I II III
A BRONX TALE I, II, III
DUFFLE BAG CARTEL I II III IV V VI
HEARTLESS GOON I II III IV V
A SAVAGE DOPEBOY I II
DRUG LORDS I II III
CUTTHROAT MAFIA I II
KING OF THE TRENCHES
By **Ghost**

LAY IT DOWN I & II
LAST OF A DYING BREED I II
BLOOD STAINS OF A SHOTTA I & II III
By **Jamaica**

LOYAL TO THE GAME I II III
LIFE OF SIN I, II III
By **TJ & Jelissa**

IF LOVING HIM IS WRONG…I & II
LOVE ME EVEN WHEN IT HURTS I II III
By **Jelissa**

PUSH IT TO THE LIMIT
By **Bre' Hayes**

BLOODY COMMAS I & II
SKI MASK CARTEL I, II & III
KING OF NEW YORK I II, III IV V
RISE TO POWER I II III
COKE KINGS I II III IV V
BORN HEARTLESS I II III IV
KING OF THE TRAP I II
By **T.J. Edwards**

WHEN THE STREETS CLAP BACK I & II III
THE HEART OF A SAVAGE I II III IV
MONEY MAFIA I II
LOYAL TO THE SOIL I II III
By **Jibril Williams**

A DISTINGUISHED THUG STOLE MY HEART I II & III
LOVE SHOULDN'T HURT I II III IV
RENEGADE BOYS 1-4
PAID IN KARMA 1-3
SAVAGE STORMS 1-3
AN UNFORESEEN LOVE 1-3
BABY, I'M WINTERTIME COLD 1-3
A THUG'S STREET PRINCESS 1&2
By **Meesha**

A GANGSTER'S CODE 1-3
A GANGSTER'S SYN 1-3
THE SAVAGE LIFE 1-3
CHAINED TO THE STREETS 1-3
BLOOD ON THE MONEY 1-3
A GANGSTA'S PAIN 1-3
BEAUTIFUL LIES AND UGLY TRUTHS
CHURCH IN THESE STREETS
By **J-Blunt**

CUM FOR ME 1-8
An LDP Erotica Collaboration

BLOOD OF A BOSS 1-5
SHADOWS OF THE GAME
TRAP BASTARD
By **Askari**

THE STREETS BLEED MURDER 1-3
THE HEART OF A GANGSTA 1-3
By **Jerry Jackson**

WHEN A GOOD GIRL GOES BAD
By **Adrienne**

THE COST OF LOYALTY 1-3
By **Kweli**

BRIDE OF A HUSTLA 1-3
THE FETTI GIRLS 1-3
CORRUPTED BY A GANGSTA 1-4
BLINDED BY HIS LOVE
THE PRICE YOU PAY FOR LOVE 1-3
DOPE GIRL MAGIC 1-3
By **Destiny Skai**

A KINGPIN'S AMBITION
A KINGPIN'S AMBITION II
I MURDER FOR THE DOUGH
By **Ambitious**

TRUE SAVAGE 1-7
DOPE BOY MAGIC 1-3
MIDNIGHT CARTEL 1-3
CITY OF KINGZ 1&2
NIGHTMARE ON SILENT AVE
THE PLUG OF LIL MEXICO 1&2
CLASSIC CITY
By **Chris Green**

A GANGSTER'S REVENGE 1-4
THE BOSS MAN'S DAUGHTERS 1-5
A SAVAGE LOVE 1&2
BAE BELONGS TO ME 1&2
A HUSTLER'S DECEIT 1-3
WHAT BAD BITCHES DO 1-3
SOUL OF A MONSTER 1-3
KILL ZONE
A DOPE BOY'S QUEEN 1-3
TIL DEATH 1-3
IMMA DIE BOUT MINE 1-4
By **Aryanna**

A DOPEBOY'S PRAYER
By **Eddie "Wolf" Lee**

THE KING CARTEL 1-3
By **Frank Gresham**

THESE NIGGAS AIN'T LOYAL 1-3
By **Nikki Tee**

GANGSTA SHYT 1-3
By **CATO**

THE ULTIMATE BETRAYAL
By **Phoenix**

BOSS'N UP 1-3
By **Royal Nicole**

I LOVE YOU TO DEATH
By **Destiny J**

I RIDE FOR MY HITTA
I STILL RIDE FOR MY HITTA
By **Misty Holt**

LOVE & CHASIN' PAPER
By **Qay Crockett**

TO DIE IN VAIN
SINS OF A HUSTLA
By **ASAD**

BROOKLYN HUSTLAZ
By **Boogsy Morina**

BROOKLYN ON LOCK 1 & 2
By **Sonovia**

GANGSTA CITY
By **Teddy Duke**

A DRUG KING AND HIS DIAMOND 1-3
A DOPEMAN'S RICHES
HER MAN, MINE'S TOO 1&2
CASH MONEY HO'S
THE WIFEY I USED TO BE 1&2
PRETTY GIRLS DO NASTY THINGS
By **Nicole Goosby**

LIPSTICK KILLAH 1-3
CRIME OF PASSION 1-3
FRIEND OR FOE 1-3
By **Mimi**

TRAPHOUSE KING 1-3
KINGPIN KILLAZ 1-3
STREET KINGS 1&2
PAID IN BLOOD 1&2
CARTEL KILLAZ 1-3
DOPE GODS 1&2
By **Hood Rich**

THE STREETS ARE CALLING
By **Duquie Wilson**

STEADY MOBBN' 1-3
THE STREETS STAINED MY SOUL 1-3
By **Marcellus Allen**

WHO SHOT YA 1-3
SON OF A DOPE FIEND 1-4
HEAVEN GOT A GHETTO 1&2
SKI MASK MONEY 1&2
By **Renta**

GORILLAZ IN THE BAY 1-4
TEARS OF A GANGSTA 1/&2
3X KRAZY 1&2
STRAIGHT BEAST MODE 1&2
By **DE'KARI**

TRIGGADALE 1-3
MURDA WAS THE CASE 1-3
By **Elijah R. Freeman**

SLAUGHTER GANG 1-3
RUTHLESS HEART 1-3
By **Willie Slaughter**

GOD BLESS THE TRAPPERS 1-3
THESE SCANDALOUS STREETS 1-3
FEAR MY GANGSTA 1-5
THESE STREETS DON'T LOVE NOBODY 1-2
BURY ME A G 1-5
A GANGSTA'S EMPIRE 1-4
THE DOPEMAN'S BODYGAURD 1&2
THE REALEST KILLAZ 1-3
THE LAST OF THE OGS 1-3
By **Tranay Adams**

MARRIED TO A BOSS 1-3
By **Destiny Skai & Chris Green**

KINGZ OF THE GAME 1-7
CRIME BOSS 1-3
By **Playa Ray**

FUK SHYT
By **Blakk Diamond**

DON'T F#CK WITH MY HEART 1&2
By **Linnea**

ADDICTED TO THE DRAMA 1-3
IN THE ARM OF HIS BOSS
By **Jamila**

LOYALTY AIN'T PROMISED 1&2
By **Keith Williams**

YAYO 1-4
A SHOOTER'S AMBITION 1&2
BRED IN THE GAME
By **S. Allen**

TRAP GOD 1-3
RICH $AVAGE 1-3
MONEY IN THE GRAVE 1-3
CARTEL MONEY
By **Martell Troublesome Bolden**

FOREVER GANGSTA 1&2
GLOCKS ON SATIN SHEETS 1&2
By **Adrian Dulan**

TOE TAGZ 1-4
LEVELS TO THIS SHYT 1&2
IT'S JUST ME AND YOU
By **Ah'Million**

KINGPIN DREAMS 1-3
RAN OFF ON DA PLUG
By **Paper Boi Rari**

THE STREETS MADE ME 1-3
By **Larry D. Wright**

CONFESSIONS OF A GANGSTA 1-4
CONFESSIONS OF A JACKBOY 1-3
CONFESSIONS OF A HITMAN
By **Nicholas Lock**

I'M NOTHING WITHOUT HIS LOVE
SINS OF A THUG
TO THE THUG I LOVED BEFORE
A GANGSTA SAVED XMAS
IN A HUSTLER I TRUST
By **Monet Dragun**

QUIET MONEY 1-3
THUG LIFE 1-3
EXTENDED CLIP 1&2
A GANGSTA'S PARADISE
By **Trai'Quan**

CAUGHT UP IN THE LIFE 1-3
THE STREETS NEVER LET GO 1-3
By **Robert Baptiste**

NEW TO THE GAME 1-3
MONEY, MURDER & MEMORIES 1-3
By **Malik D. Rice**

CREAM 2-3
THE STREETS WILL TALK
By **Yolanda Moore**

THE STREETS WILL NEVER CLOSE 1-3
By **K'ajji**

LIFE OF A SAVAGE 1-4
A GANGSTA'S QUR'AN 1-4
MURDA SEASON 1-3
GANGLAND CARTEL 1-3
CHI'RAQ GANGSTAS 1-4
KILLERS ON ELM STREET 1-3
JACK BOYZ N DA BRONX 1-3
A DOPEBOY'S DREAM 1-3
JACK BOYS VS DOPE BOYS 1-3
COKE GIRLZ
COKE BOYS
SOSA GANG 1&2
BRONX SAVAGES
BODYMORE KINGPINS
BLOOD OF A GOON
By **Romell Tukes**

CONCRETE KILLA 1-3
VICIOUS LOYALTY 1-3
By **Kingpen**

THE ULTIMATE SACRIFICE 1-6
KHADIFI
IF YOU CROSS ME ONCE 1-3
ANGEL 1-4
IN THE BLINK OF AN EYE
By **Anthony Fields**

THE LIFE OF A HOOD STAR
By **Ca$h & Rashia Wilson**

NIGHTMARES OF A HUSTLA 1-3
BLOOD AND GAMES 1&2
By **King Dream**

GHOST MOB
By **Stilloan Robinson**

HARD AND RUTHLESS 1&2
MOB TOWN 251
THE BILLIONAIRE BENTLEYS 1-3
REAL G'S MOVE IN SILENCE
By **Von Diesel**

MOB TIES 1-7
SOUL OF A HUSTLER, HEART OF A KILLER 1-3
GORILLAZ IN THE TRENCHES
By **SayNoMore**

BODYMORE MURDERLAND 1-3
THE BIRTH OF A GANGSTER 1-4
By **Delmont Player**

FOR THE LOVE OF A BOSS 1&2
By **C. D. Blue**

KILLA KOUNTY 1-5
By **Khufu**

MOBBED UP 1-4
THE BRICK MAN 1-5
THE COCAINE PRINCESS 1-10
STEPPERS 1-3
SUPER GREMLIN 1-4
By **King Rio**

MONEY GAME 1&2
By **Smoove Dolla**

A GANGSTA'S KARMA 1-4
By **FLAME**

KING OF THE TRENCHES 1-3
By **GHOST & TRANAY ADAMS**

GUNS DOWN, BOTTOMS UP! | LO-LIFE

QUEEN OF THE ZOO 1&2
By **Black Migo**

GRIMEY WAYS 1-3
BETRAYAL OF A G
By **Ray Vinci**

XMAS WITH AN ATL SHOOTER
By **Ca$h & Destiny Skai**

KING KILLA 1&2
By **Vincent "Vitto" Holloway**

BETRAYAL OF A THUG 1&2
By **Fre$h**

THE MURDER QUEENS 1-5
By **Michael Gallon**

FOR THE LOVE OF BLOOD 1-4
By **Jamel Mitchell**

HOOD CONSIGLIERE 1&2
NO TIME FOR ERROR
By **Keese**

PROTÉGÉ OF A LEGEND 1&2
LOVE IN THE TRENCHES 1&2
By **Corey Robinson**

THE PLUG'S RUTHLESS DAUGHTER
By **Tony Daniels**

BORN IN THE GRAVE 1-3
CRIME PAYS
By **Self Made Tay**

MOAN IN MY MOUTH
By **XTASY**

TORN BETWEEN A GANGSTER AND A GENTLEMAN
By **J-BLUNT & Miss Kim**

LOYALTY IS EVERYTHING 1-3
CITY OF SMOKE 1&2
By **Molotti**

HERE TODAY GONE TOMORROW 1&2
By **Fly Rock**

WOMEN LIE MEN LIE 1-4
FIFTY SHADES OF SNOW 1-3
STACK BEFORE YOU SPLURGE
GIRLS FALL LIKE DOMINOES
NAÏVE TO THE STREETS
By **ROY MILLIGAN**

PILLOW PRINCESS
By **S. Hawkins**

THE BUTTERFLY MAFIA 1-3
SALUTE MY SAVAGERY 1&2
By **Fumiya Payne**

THE LANE 1&2
By Ken-Ken Spence

THE PUSSY TRAP 1-5
By **Nene Capri**

DIRTY DNA
By **Blaque**

SANCTIFIED AND HORNY
by **XTASY**

BOOKS BY LDP'S CEO, CA$H

TRUST IN NO MAN
TRUST IN NO MAN 2
TRUST IN NO MAN 3
BONDED BY BLOOD
SHORTY GOT A THUG
THUGS CRY
THUGS CRY 2
THUGS CRY 3
TRUST NO BITCH
TRUST NO BITCH 2
TRUST NO BITCH 3
TIL MY CASKET DROPS
RESTRAINING ORDER
RESTRAINING ORDER 2
IN LOVE WITH A CONVICT
LIFE OF A HOOD STAR
XMAS WITH AN ATL SHOOTER